PERFECT MATCHA

A BOLD BREW NOVEL

ERIN MCLELLAN

ISBN 978-1-7350049-4-5

Ebook ASIN B08T7TVHBR

Editing: Edie Danford

Proofreading: Susan Selva, https://www.lescourtauthorservices.com

Cover Artist: Cate Ashwood, http://www.cateashwooddesigns.com

After years of focusing on his career, Theodore Punch is tired of being alone. But landing a good man isn't easy. When Theo needs a date for an ex-boyfriend's wedding, he knows just the solution—a matchmaker. And there's no better matchmaker than his social butterfly best friend, Camden Ray.

There's only one problem: Camden has been in love with Theo for half their lives but doesn't have the guts to come clean. Camden will do anything to make Theo happy, even if it hurts, and he already has a match for Theo in mind— his boss, the handsome owner of the local adult novelty shop.

Now there's another problem: Theo has zero experience with toys. Luckily, Camden is only a phone call away and more than happy to walk Theo through naughty gadget lessons. Spicy phone calls, a dash of role play, and a load of pesky emotions brew between them. It's not the match either of them intended but could be the perfect solution to all their problems, if their friendship can survive the infusion of feelings.

Perfect Matcha is 35k words of friends-to-lovers, matchmaking fun with plenty of steam. It's part of the multi-author Bold Brew universe centered on an inclusive coffee shop in a fictional city. Each Bold Brew story can be enjoyed as a stand-alone.

To my perfect match and best pandemic partner ever

CONTENT WARNINGS

Perfect Matcha is a light-hearted novella, but there are some content warnings readers might want to be aware of:

Explicit language; alcohol consumption; explicit sex, including phone sex, use of toys, and lite role play. Role play scenarios include the main characters pretending to be boss/employee, professor/student, strangers, and card counter/casino bodyguard.

For more information on these content warnings, including chapter designations for the role play scenes, visit erinmclellan.com.

CHAPTER ONE

CAMDEN WAS LATE. He knocked the dirty, slushy snow off his work boots outside the door of Bold Brew. The bottoms of his pantlegs were soaked and heavy, and his fingers hurt from the cold. The warmth of the coffee shop would be nice after a long day outside, as would the calm that came from spending a few hours with Theo.

Goofy, nerdy, perfect Theodore Punch.

His best friend. The most important person in his life.

The man of his dreams, but Camden didn't have the guts to tell Theo that.

Maybe today would be the day. Maybe he would open that coffee shop door, stride over to their table, grab Theo's baffled face, and lay one on him.

Or maybe not.

Spoiler alert—Camden Ray was a chickenshit.

The scent of espresso and hearty food snapped

Camden out of his daydreaming, and the door jangled closed behind him. Theo looked up at the sound of the door, a crooked smile blooming on his face.

Yeah, Camden was in love with that man, but he'd seen firsthand the pain a failed romantic relationship with your best friend could wreak. And so had Theo.

"Whatcha got for me today?" Camden asked. There were two steaming mugs on the table.

Theo grinned and snapped his laptop shut. "Taste it and find out."

Before sitting down, Camden tousled Theo's hair for long enough to tighten his own chest but not so long that it seemed romantic. Camden had these small, platonic gestures down. They fed his pathetic heart, and Theo, who'd grown up in a family that exemplified the definition of *cold*, ate up any show of demonstrative friendship.

When they were children, Theo had always been down for hugging or wrestling as their little pack, the Three Mountaineers—a play on the Three Musketeers because they lived on a ridge—ran roughshod through the neighborhood's forest and hills. Camden, and their other best friend, Freddie, had been happy to oblige.

Camden was still happy to oblige.

Camden lifted the large mug to his face and sniffed. "Hot chocolate."

It was common for Theo to get him drinks that were

too sugary because Theo liked to steal sips of them, but hot chocolate didn't sound half-bad.

"With a kick." Theo took a sip of his own drink, which was his usual matcha with honey. He'd probably already had three that day. He drank so much of it that if Camden got close enough, he swore he could smell the tea's grassy earthiness on Theo's skin.

The chocolate slipped over Camden's tongue and something spicy, maybe cayenne, hit him in the back of the throat after he swallowed. It wasn't the plain black coffee he would have chosen for himself, but it tasted pretty amazing on a cold, dreary day.

"Theodore, here's your food order," the pink-haired barista called from the counter. The guy gave Theo a wink as he retrieved his food.

Camden couldn't hold in his smile. Theo was a regular here. He supposed they both were, but Theo finding community at this funky coffee shop made Camden's heart abnormally happy since Theo was such an introvert. Bold Brew was a good place. It was a bit of a hub for Laurelsburg's queer and kink communities, but it was also just a great strong-brew coffee shop.

Theo returned to the table with a plate of ham and cheese sliders on buttery Hawaiian sweet rolls. Camden's mouth watered.

"How was work?" Theo asked after they'd both

devoured one slider apiece. "You're all coveralled up today. Very manly."

"I wear this to work every day." Camden had started working thirty hours a week as a groundskeeper for Laurelsburg University at the beginning of the winter. It was hard work, but Camden enjoyed being outside.

He was hoping they'd want to keep him on through the spring and summer. He liked the idea of mowing the green, green grass in front of the library and planting flowers near the student union. Laurelsburg had a beautiful campus, and helping create some of that beauty appealed to him. He'd had a shit-ton of crappy jobs, but groundskeeper wasn't one of them.

"You don't wear those coveralls to First-Rate Finishes, do you?" Theo's voice was full of an ornery quality that made Camden's heart race.

"No."

"I bet you'd sell more vibrators if you did."

Camden concealed his laughter by taking a sip of his hot chocolate and fishing a slider off the plate.

"What *do* you wear at the sex-toy shop?" Theo asked with not-so-feigned innocence.

"I wear my regular clothes." Camden had recently picked up weekend hours at First-Rate Finishes, a local adult novelty boutique, because the owner, Hawke, was a gem who liked helping out his friends. "You'd know if you ever visited me there."

Between the two jobs, Camden was finally earning enough for rent *and* to make a dent in his useless student loans.

A distinctly rosy tint spread up Theo's angular cheekbones, making the spray of freckles on his nose more pronounced. Camden ate up the sight like a piece of cake. He loved the way Theo looked. Loved his dark, messy curls and silvery-blue eyes. Loved his hipster, wire-rimmed glasses and his earnest smile. Theo's face had always been precious to Camden, but he could hardly think straight when Theo blushed.

"If I want to see you in ratty sweatpants and an ancient Laurelsburg U shirt, I can just show up at your place any old time."

Camden laughed and somehow resisted the urge to reach across the table and ruffle Theo's hair again. Barely. "So, how's your week going?"

Theo sighed theatrically and took a huge gulp of his tea. "Horribly."

"Uh-oh. Big drama in the bioinformatics world again?" Camden didn't quite understand Theo's data-science job but enjoyed listening to him talk all smart and nerdy about it.

"Yeah, actually. You would not believe what happened at our last team-building event. But that's not the horrible thing. I got assigned a boring last-minute project with a ridiculous deadline. Plus, this awful weather means I can't ride my bike, so I'm stuck driving on icy roads or taking the bus." He grabbed Camden's hot chocolate and tasted it. "Oh, that's yummy. Switch."

Camden allowed Theo to commandeer his drink but caught his wrist as Theo tried to push his tea across the table. Theo would want the rest of his own drink once the hot chocolate was gone.

"What else?" Camden asked. Bad things came in threes.

Theo stared down at where Camden still had a hold on him. "I got the wedding invite."

Camden tensed, guilt hitting him in a wave. He should have been able to prepare Theo for that, protect him. Protecting Theo, being there for him through thick and thin, had always been Camden's job.

Memories flooded his brain.

The three of them as children—Camden, Theo, and Freddie—running up a hill in their Halloween costumes, plastic pumpkins full of cheap candy in their hands. Theo tripping over his hem and Camden catching him.

As teenagers, hiding in the woods with pot and wine coolers Freddie had stolen from his mom, confessing their deepest, most private secrets. Camden assuring Theo it was okay to want to kiss boys.

As college freshmen, together at a Pride mixer, Freddie's eyes trained on Theo as he moved through the crowd.

Then, after Camden had dropped out junior year, Theo calling him late at night, drunk and complaining about Freddie's boyfriend.

At brunch years later, when Theo got up to go to the restroom and Freddie leaned over to admit he was going to do it; he was going to tell Theo how he felt.

Seeing Freddie and Theo kiss for the first time during a dinner party.

Camden realizing over canapes that he'd missed his chance, that he'd waited too long, thinking he'd have all the time in the world once he'd grown up a little.

Theo showing up at Camden's apartment the week of his dissertation defense absolutely wrecked because Freddie had left him, their friendship not strong enough to save their love.

Last year, Freddie introducing Camden to his new fiancé and asking Camden to be a groomsman.

Years and years and years of history. From inseparable to broken, unable to be in a room together.

Last Camden had heard, Freddie had been on the fence about inviting Theo to the wedding at all.

Camden squeezed Theo's wrist, then let it go. "That's ... shitty."

Theo finished Camden's hot chocolate in one long drink. "Don't humor me. I'm just in my feelings. And I'm happy for him. He deserves a great partner and a happy marriage." He nudged his glasses higher on the bridge of his nose.

"You're allowed to have feelings about it, Theo."

Theo smiled weakly. "Not sure why it's put me in such a weird mood. We broke up five years ago."

"You were together for three. That's a long time."

Three years, two months, and ten days. Not that Camden had kept track or anything.

Theo hadn't been in a relationship since.

Not that Camden had kept track of that either.

"But I was buried under my own doctoral bullshit that whole time. We were glorified roommates who sometimes cuddled and rarely had sex because I was too busy and self-absorbed and—"

"Hey, whoa, Theo. It's all right. The breakup wasn't your fault."

People broke up. That was life.

Camden's fear was about what had happened to Theo and Freddie *after* their breakup. They'd been incapable of being in the same room without awkwardness, incapable of smiling at each other without sadness. Every conversation was tense and dysfunctional until they'd eventually stopped trying. Theo and Freddie's decades-old friendship had warped into something ugly and small. An afterthought. A cell in the *maybe* column of a wedding invite list.

That terrified Camden. He couldn't imagine a life

without Theo's friendship, a life where their connection was relegated to bittersweet memories.

That fear was what made it essential for Camden to push down his feelings for Theo, to keep them a secret. It wasn't worth the risk.

"I know what will cheer you up," Camden said, ready to suggest Tex-Mex, beer, and a game of shuffleboard, but Theo cut him off.

"A date! To the wedding. That's what I need. Someone cool." Theo blinked at Camden a few times, his eyes owlish behind his glasses. "*You* know cool people."

CHAPTER TWO

"I HAVE THE BEST IDEAS," Theo said, marveling at himself. Why had he never thought of this before? Everything was clicking into place, like a perfect algorithm.

Camden Ray was Mr. Social Circle. He had all kinds of friends, which was mystifying to Theo as someone who had basically only ever had two. One of whom he'd dated then neglected during the most stressful time of his life, so for real, Theo had *one* friend. And *one* ex-boyfriend.

But Camden ... he *knew* people. He was keyed into the queer spaces in town, and some of the kink ones too, which they did not speak about because Theo was an awkward prude.

"Who is your coolest single friend?" Theo asked. He grabbed Camden's hot-chocolate mug to take another drink, only to remember he'd already downed it, so he seized the last heavenly ham sandwich thing instead.

Camden pushed Theo's tea into his hand. "Umm. Here."

Theo drank it greedily. Good ideas made him thirsty. "Freddie's wedding is in two months." The words tasted bitter on Theo's tongue.

"And you actually want to go?"

"Of course. Maybe it'll be weird, but we've been friends since we were seven. The Three Mountaineers should be at each other's weddings, don't you think?"

"I guess."

The breakup with Freddie had definitely been Theo's fault, regardless of what Camden thought. Theo had missed birthdays and special dinners. He'd slept through movie nights and eaten meals like an automaton. He'd been unavailable—physically, emotionally, in all the ways.

He used to wonder what would have happened if he and Freddie had waited to get together until after Theo finished school, but years and years of reflection kept bringing Theo back to one little problem.

He hadn't loved Freddie.

He hadn't allowed himself to.

Theo would never have been able to crack himself open and wear his heart as a necklace for the whole world to see. Or for *Freddie* to see. That was what Freddie had needed. What he deserved. Someone present, someone willing to be vulnerable. Someone to sing love songs to on the internet and celebrate with flash mobs in the town square. Freddie had found that person—they had a whole-ass YouTube channel together—and Theo was genuinely happy for him.

"What are you asking for exactly?" Camden said.

"A date."

"Go with me. Be my date. It'll be fun."

Theo scoffed and waved that away. "My best friend bestowing a pity date on me for a wedding isn't exactly the vibe I'm going for here."

Not that Camden wouldn't strike a fine figure at a wedding. He was all golden skin and chiseled jaw and working-man muscles. Theo was used to Camden's ridiculous level of handsomeness and tended to disregard his looks as unimportant. Plus, he remembered the awkward teen years before Camden grew into his ears.

"It's not a pity date," Camden said, snapping Theo out of his blurry-eyed contemplation of the way Camden's forearms looked like part of an ad for mail-order lumberjacks. "It could be real ... Or we could pretend it's real. I could hold your hand and kiss you and stuff."

"A fake date for the wedding." Theo scratched his chin, considering it, even though it was a bizarre and untenable suggestion. And what would they do after the wedding? Stage a breakup but continue to hang out several times a week? It made no sense, and Freddie would see right through it, which wasn't ideal. Theo wanted Freddie to see him thriving. "Let's save that as a last resort. Plus, aren't you a groomsman? You'll be busy."

Camden frowned. "Then, what? You want a boyfriend? A fuck buddy? A fake date for the wedding who is *not* me. I need some stipulations if I'm going to play matchmaker."

"Well ... a boyfriend would be nice." Obviously, Theo wanted a boyfriend. Someone to share the enchilada plate at his favorite Mexican restaurant. Someone who would lose boardgames to him. Someone to cuddle up with while watching action movies. Someone to share cozy coffee shop dates. *Sign him up.*

It was the other parts of a relationship that were difficult. The letting himself be truly seen by a human who wasn't the human sitting across the table from him at this very moment. *That* was the issue. *That* was why it'd been so easy for him to push off relationships for years and bury himself in work.

But now he had his diplomas and an established career. He was ready for a relationship. He just needed help finding a man, and who better to help with that pursuit than Camden?

"A boyfriend." Camden grimaced around the word, which was no surprise. He'd never seemed interested in relationships.

"Yeah. Or the possibility of one. I don't want a fuck

buddy or a fake date." Theo traced a scratch in the tabletop. "I don't want to be lonely anymore."

"So in this scenario, I set you up with 'someone cool,' you hit it off, you fall in love, you show up to Freddie O'Neil's wedding full of new-relationship glow."

"Yeah, easy peasy."

Camden's face was tight. "Sure. Who do you have in mind?"

"I don't have anyone in mind!" Theo said, flushing slightly. "That's the point. You know your friends better than me."

Theo waited as Camden internally scrolled through his eminently large Rolodex of friends, firing off names out loud, then rejecting them before Theo could respond.

Then, just as swiftly, Camden froze, his body going still. He shifted his gaze to Theo and said, "Hawke Howard."

Theo waited, positive that Camden was going to change his mind like he had with the other suggestions. When he didn't, Theo's brain stuttered and seemed to short out. "You want to set me up with your sex-toy boss?"

"Don't call him my sex-toy boss." Camden laughed sharply. "He loves animals and his family. He owns his own business and has an adorable house. He's career focused like you. He's smart enough to keep up when you talk about your job. He's cute."

"Cute is an understatement."

"Yeah." Camden smiled. Or grimaced. Theo couldn't tell. "He's sexy, frankly. Open and kind. He's told me he's ready to settle down. He'd treat you well."

"And he has tattoos." This suggestion was blowing Theo's mind. Hawke Howard was too good for him. But it was also incredibly enticing to imagine waltzing into Freddie's wedding—hell, *anyone's* wedding—with Hawke on his arm.

"Yes."

"And piercings."

"Only on his face."

Theo gawped at Camden. "How do you know that? Have you seen him naked?"

Camden rolled his eyes. "I haven't had sex with Hawke, if that's what you're implying. But, yes, I saw him naked at a house party of sorts. Well, it was at a mansion but same thing."

"Hawke goes to *sex parties*?" Theo hated how squeaky his voice sounded. He wasn't inexperienced per se. He'd had some practice. But not sex-party-level practice. "Wait ... *you* go to sex parties?"

"Not recently. It wasn't my thing. Maybe if I went with a partner, I would like it more, but—"

"Cam, I can't date a guy who goes to sex parties!" Theo whisper-screamed.

"I think the term is 'play parties.' And you already said *no* to me."

Theo groaned. "Not you! *Hawke.* I can't date a man who goes to play parties and owns a fancy sex-toy shop and has all this ... all this ..." Theo waved his hand like he was dialing a rotary phone. His pulse was buzzing in his ears.

Camden grabbed his fingers. "Hey. Are you being a snob?" he asked gently.

"What? No!" A dude at a nearby table turned to glare at them, so Theo dropped his voice. "Hawke Howard is so out of my league. I wanted you to choose someone cool, not someone untouchable."

A muscle ticked in Camden's stubbly jaw. "You're the best person I know. Hawke would be lucky to date you. Don't be mean to yourself."

Some of Theo's panic melted away at Camden's words. The way Camden was cradling Theo's hand in his palms didn't hurt either, but Camden's hands were cold. Theo needed to research winter work gloves. There were all kinds of fancy technical performance fabrics out there, and Theo knew Camden wouldn't splurge on himself.

Camden opened his mouth a few times like he was reluctant to say what he was about to say. Finally, he hissed out, "I happen to know that Hawke thinks you're attractive. He asks about you. Often. I'm pretty sure he'd be interested."

"Oh." Theo clutched at Camden's fingers. "I've never

even used a sex toy, Cam. Or owned one. Or held one. That would be like dating a groundskeeper without ever having gone outside. How the hell am I supposed to date Hawke Howard?"

A burst of fierceness fired through Camden's eyes. "Oh, Theodore, I can help with that."

CHAPTER THREE

CAMDEN HAD REALLY STEPPED in it today. What the hell had he been thinking, offering to set Theo up with Hawke Howard of all people?

After a bit of back and forth, they'd decided that Theo would try some sex toys, helpfully curated by Camden. Once Theo was comfortable, or at least not a total newb, Camden would arrange a date for Theo and Hawke. The wedding wasn't for two months. Plenty of time.

Camden fell back on his bed with a groan and placed his cell, speakerphone on, on his chest.

"You're going to *what?* Buy him a welcome-to-sex-toys gift basket, then play matchmaker between him and one of the nicest, coolest, hottest men in Laurelsburg?" Camden's twin sister, Cassie, asked, not so much commiserating, but crowing about Camden's hopelessness.

Camden had made a huge mistake sending her a link

to Hawke's Instagram. It was full of unintentional thirst traps. One of the nice things about Hawke was that he seemed to be unaware of his own appeal. Much like Theo, actually. They were perfect for each other.

Blech.

"Don't forget successful. Or artistic. Or exciting," Camden said.

"Ah yes. And hung ... Probably."

Camden laughed. "Yeah. Probably." *Definitely.*

"You're a glutton for punishment. You're setting up the man you love with someone who is—"

"*Way* better for him than me, yes." Camden scrubbed a hand over his face.

It wasn't only that he was worried about ruining the most important relationship in his life. He was also a bit of a mess. It was an age-old story. Golden boy athlete turned frat boy who slept and partied his way through Greek row —sororities and fraternities—turned college dropout turned underemployed asshole. His life was just now getting on track, at thirty years old, but only because he'd been lucky enough to find two jobs with compatible schedules.

"Oh, fuck off, Camden. You'd be great for Theo."

A heavy bass beat thumped through Camden's floors, reminding him he lived in a trash-hole apartment building full of partying college kids.

"Theo has his shit together, sis. I do not."

"Shit-having is relative. You say I have my shit together, but I got drunk and left my wallet and a whole-ass stiletto, only *one* of them, in a hookup's apartment last night. Having a steady job and a nice apartment does not make you less of a mess."

"Did you get your stuff back?" Camden asked. He tried not to be the defensive older brother, mostly because Cassie had always been way better at life than him, but sometimes she made it hard to refrain.

"Yeah. She texted me this morning. We have a second date ... in an hour." Cassie laughed, and the sound made him smile. "You'd be good for Theo because you love him and understand him. You'll be gentle with his heart."

And there went Camden's smile. His sister had no idea how her words hurt. "Hawke would be gentle too. He's a good guy. One of the best. Plus, you know what happened between Freddie and Theo. What would I do if I lost Theo because I couldn't keep my mushy emotions to myself? It would feel like losing everything in my life that's worth having."

"I hate that you don't see yourself clearly. I get that it's scary and that you might not want to risk losing Theo's friendship, but for Christ's sake, Camden, you don't have to tear yourself apart by hand delivering him to a Prince Charming either."

"I know," he said. "I do, but I promised. I don't want Theo to walk into that wedding alone. He deserves to walk in with his head held high and an amazing person on his arm. And that person cannot be me."

"Fine." Cassie sighed a sigh so reminiscent of their childhood that it made him miss her even more. "What are you going to put in the gift basket, then?"

"Just the normal stuff."

"What's normal?" she asked all faux naivety. She aimed to embarrass him. Typical sibling shit.

"I'm not having this conversation with you."

"You sell sex toys, Camden. Surely you talk about them at work."

"Yeah, but the customers aren't my little sister."

"Don't call me little. You're only older by twenty minutes." She continued to razz him, and he took it because that was how their relationship worked. Eventually, she had to go so she wouldn't be late for her date.

He missed his sister. She kept him grounded, but she lived in Philadelphia and worked as a flight attendant. They didn't see each other as often as he would have liked. They'd grown up in a small town an hour away from Laurelsburg, and he'd settled into Laurelsburg with no desire to ever leave. Cassie, on the other hand, had the wanderlust bug. He'd been lucky to catch her on the phone tonight.

His brain was stuck on her comments about his gift-basket idea. He really did want Theo to feel relaxed with

Hawke, and Camden believed that most people could benefit from a thoughtful sex toy. It also appealed to Camden's caveman impulses to introduce Theo to toys, but he was purposefully ignoring all inner chest beating. Cassie thought he was foolish to set Theo up with Hawke, but Camden wanted Theo to be happy.

Hawke would be an awesome partner for him. Theo needed someone who was ambitious and settled. Hawke needed someone who was loyal and sweet.

No one was as loyal as Theodore Punch. He bought his bike gear from the old cycle shop across town rather than the new one closer to his apartment. He refused to go to Starbucks because of his fidelity to Bold Brew. He never, not once, turned his back on Camden while Camden was partying his way toward failing out of college.

When Theo decided you were his person, you were his person for life.

So yeah, it would slowly shred Camden's heart to pieces if Theo fell for Hawke, but he also knew setting them up was the right thing to do. If it would make Theo happy, Camden would move mountains.

It might take moving the Alleghenies to get Theo comfortable with sex toys, but Camden was willing to try. He didn't actually think Theo needed experience on this front to be with Hawke. Hawke was calm and understanding, and Camden had a hard time believing

Theo's sex-toy preferences, or lack thereof, would have any effect on Hawke's affection or attraction to him.

But Theo seemed to think it would give him peace of mind, so the next day, after work, Camden drove through the slick streets to make a gift basket for his friend.

The bell over the door of First-Rate Finishes jingled as Camden walked in. There were only two other customers inside—Joe and Levi, semiregulars who could usually be found in the lingerie section. He smiled at them as he moved farther into the store. His coworker, Diana, was behind the counter reading a worn paperback romance. Camden loved Diana. She was a pro at cosplay, rocked at customer service, could drink him under the table, and was adorably in love with her wife. He'd been their third once, years ago, and it had been fun, athletic, and perfectly unemotional.

"Well, if it isn't my favorite lug nut," she said as he approached the register. Today she had on a cropped sweater showing off her dark skin and soft curves. "What are you doing here? You're not on the schedule until Saturday."

"Buying a few presents for a friend. Did we get in the new shipment of Fleshstrokers from Lady Robin's Intimate Implements?" That was Camden's favorite brand.

"Yes. They're beautiful too. I stocked them this afternoon."

"Thanks." He turned toward the corner of the shop

where Hawke kept the masturbation sleeves and other toys specifically for dicks. He could see the Lady Robin's steampunk marketing front and center.

"You're welcome. Let me know if you have any questions," Diana called to him. He grinned at her over his shoulder.

First-Rate Finishes was a boutique-style shop with very well-curated stock. The space was full of reclaimed wood and brushed-metal shelves with vintage light fixtures. As much as he appreciated an industrial-chic aesthetic, it was the people who worked and shopped there who made the place special.

Within a few minutes, Camden had filled his arms with a number of items he thought would be suitable for a beginner. Diana skipped over with a wire bin. He gratefully unloaded his haul into it. It was full to bursting.

She fingered through the boxes curiously. "You haven't picked out any prostate massagers yet."

He sighed. "I'm going to need a bigger basket."

"Good thing we get an employee discount."

Definitely a good thing. He might have to forgo takeout this month or cancel one of his streaming services, but it would be a small fortune well spent.

CHAPTER FOUR

IT HAD BEEN three days since Theo had asked Camden to play matchmaker and Camden had suggested Hawke Howard.

Three days for Theo to think about trying to have a conversation with Hawke without making a fool of himself.

Three whole days to contemplate the implications of dating, and possibly, *hopefully*, eventually being intimate with Hawke.

It was intimidating. And scary.

And exciting. But mostly intimidating.

He couldn't stop thinking about it, even though he should have been thinking about the problem he'd discovered in a dataset this morning. Normally, Theo was very capable of getting in a productivity groove with the bustle of Bold Brew around him. Today, though, all the tables near him were occupied by disastrous first dates, and he couldn't stop worrying about his future disastrous first date with Hawke.

For example, at the table to his right, some airhead college boy kept offering his gluten-intolerant date bites of his cinnamon roll, despite the man's explanations. And to his left, a shy woman had accidentally spilled *two* separate drinks in her nervousness, one of them into the lap of the bewildered man across the table from her. Theo felt like these dates were a literal horoscope of his future.

The bell over the door jingled, and Theo glanced over. He hadn't expected to see Camden waltz through but happily welcomed the distraction. Camden dropped into the seat across from him.

"Hi." Theo checked the time. Then the date on the calendar. "Did we have plans?" It wasn't unusual for him to blank on stuff when he was really invested in work, which had frustrated Freddie to no end. Not that Theo was super-invested in his super-boring work project. He was basically just obsessing over the mere idea of talking to Hawke Howard without melting into an insecure puddle.

"No. I saw your fancy Prius out there on my way home from work, so I stopped by. I have a gift for you."

Theo *loved* presents. "What is it?" He sat up straighter in his seat and grinned. "Give it to me."

A strange and hungry light passed through Camden's eyes, but Theo had long ago stopped trying to interpret other people's idiosyncrasies.

"I can't give it to you here. Bundle up, and we can move it from my truck to your car."

"Is it big?"

Camden laughed. "Some of it."

"Huh?"

He scooted his seat over and whispered directly into Theo's ear. "I told you I'd help with your sex-toy uncertainty, so I have a *gift for you in my truck*. From First-Rate Finishes. For you. In my truck."

"Oh ... *Oh!*" Theo's face flamed. "Well, my goodness. Okay. I guess we better do a discreet handoff."

Theo snagged a regular named Charlie, who was hanging out at the counter, and asked him to watch his laptop and bag. Charlie seemed to take to the task with an over-serious sense of responsibility, so Theo followed Camden into the parking lot.

Luckily, Camden had parked his rusty old truck next to Theo's car. Camden opened the door to his extended cab and passed over a large basket wrapped in rose-gold cellophane and tied at the top with a silver bow. It looked like something you'd get from the Hallmark store.

Until you peeked inside.

It was cold outside, but Theo felt as if someone had poured lava on his chest. And cheeks. And ears. He deposited the basket of debauchery into his backseat and loosened his scarf.

"This is a lot of stuff," he choked out.

"Yeah."

"And I'm supposed to know what to do with it all?"

"Well, there are usually instructions in or on the box." Camden shrugged, all calm, cool, and nonchalant, like he was saying, *Oh no big deal, here's a boat load of sexy gadgets, have fun, my clueless friend.* "Plus, you could search the name of the toy on a porn site. Or ask me. Also, follow the instructions for cleaning before and after use and use the right type of lube."

"The right type of ... of, uh ..." Theo lowered his voice. "Lube?"

"Yeah. There are certain kinds that you can't use with silicone toys, and there is a lot of silicone in that basket," Camden said. *Loudly.* Okay it wasn't loud, but it *felt* loud. "What kind of lube do you use? I mean, I put some in the basket too, so you should be set, but I'm sure you have a preference."

Theo's ears started to ring. It wasn't like he and Camden had never talked about sex. As teenagers, Camden had regaled Theo and Freddie with his escapades, most of which had probably been exaggerated. And when Theo had lost his V-card sophomore year of college to a guy from the basketball team, Camden had been his first call. Camden, then Freddie. Camden had *whooped* and asked for the dirty details, which Theo had primly not provided. Freddie had pushed condoms on Theo with a frown, which had been annoying. Theo had snagged his own handful of condoms from his RA the day before because he wasn't irresponsible, thank you very much.

But now that they were older, and sex no longer felt like a new and wild discovery, they never spoke about the nitty-gritty, so Camden asking about his lube predilections was blowing Theo's mind.

"You bought me lube?" Theo whispered.

"Yeah." Camden's cheeks were very pink from the brisk cold, and Theo would have thought he looked adorable if he'd been able to think about anything but personal lubricant.

"Well, umm." Theo decided to be gracious and ignore how very weird this was. "Thank you, Cam. How much do I owe you?"

A beat of silence followed his words, and Camden frowned. "Nothing. I told you. It's a gift."

"This is an expensive gift. Are you sure?" Camden didn't make a ton of money. That wasn't a secret, and Theo hated the idea of putting him out.

"Yes. Very sure."

This was one of the nicest, most generous presents anyone had ever given Theo. Though he was wholly unprepared to take the cellophane off the basket.

Conflicting emotions bubbled up inside him, and he had no idea where to direct them, so he pointed his body at Camden and launched himself into a hug. Camden caught him with an *oomph* and held him hesitantly. It was gentle, this hug, which fucked with Theo's emotions even more.

"Thanks," he said, his mouth buried in Camden's shoulder. "I'm very nervous about all this, but thank you. You're the best matchmaker ever. Really going above and beyond."

Camden lightly touched the back of Theo's head, sending an odd ache down Theo's spine. He jerked out of the hug before he made it weird.

"You're welcome," Camden said. "And don't be nervous. I'm just a phone call away if you need me."

CHAPTER FIVE

THEO MADE it home in a daze after retrieving his laptop from Charlie. It was near the end of the workday anyway, and he wasn't going to get any statistical analysis done knowing he had hundreds of dollars of high-quality sex toys waiting for him in his vehicle. His brain was a fog of horniness and disbelief.

He worked up the nerve to untie the bow on the gift basket and let the cellophane fall where it may. The labels on the toys jumped out like comic-book bubbles.

Vibrating Butt Plug!

Zip!

Dildo!

Pow!

Nipple Clamps!

Boom!

He turned on his heels and poured himself a shot from

a bottle of tequila that had been in his pantry for eons. He wondered idly if tequila went bad, but as he grimaced through the taste, he decided he wouldn't have been able to tell either way.

Once the burn of alcohol was in his system, he returned to the basket. Someone had taken great pains to arrange the toys in a pleasant array. It looked nice enough to be on Instagram, like those pictures of fancy charcuterie boards. Only it was sex toys, not meat and cheese.

His phone buzzed right as he was reaching for something named the Monster Me Ice Zombie Dildo. A text from Camden. He opened his messages to see one that read: *Just have fun. Don't think too hard about it.*

As if.

Thinking hard about stuff was literally Theo's strong suit. It was his modus operandi. To be honest, it was one of the reasons he had trouble calming down during sex. His brain whirred and whirred and whirred with insecurities and discomfort and exasperation until it was over. He assumed most people could shut off their internal monologues during sex. That their brains went fabulously blank from pleasure, and they didn't worry about where to put their hands or if their breath smelled bad or whether the next-door neighbor would hear them when she took her shih tzu for a walk.

Another message from Camden came through.

Camden: *Start with the Fleshstroker. It's easy and intuitive. A great starter for a beginner.*

Theo grabbed the Fleshstroker. The box was made from very sturdy, luxe cardboard, which Theo could appreciate. He loved a good box.

He read the information on the back panel before opening it. His lips were tingling and his hands shaking, which was silly. It was just a masturbation sleeve. It wasn't going to bite him or anything. There weren't teeth in there.

He pulled the toy out of a plastic covering and cleaned it according to the specifications in the instructions. It was shaped like a flashlight with a sparkly pattern meant to mimic a galaxy on the shell. The end, where the lightbulb would have been if it weren't a sex toy, was navy blue and pillowy to the touch with a little hole in the middle. He dipped his finger in, and the material gave.

Okay. He could do this. It felt pleasant on his finger. He liked fucking. That was all this was. He'd fuck this interstellar flashlight thing, and it would be ... swell.

He sat at the kitchen table and unbuckled his chinos.

No. Wait. He ate at the table. He couldn't orgasm there. That would be mixed messaging. Or something.

Maybe the couch would be better. In a few short strides, he was in the living room. That was the benefit of living in an apartment—efficiency.

He plopped down on the couch and stared at the Fleshstroker.

Yep. It was time. Any minute now.

His body thought it was time. His dick was hard, and his blood was thrumming sweetly. He placed the Fleshstroker on the crown of his cock and tried to press down.

"Ow." He yanked the toy away. It had pulled at the sensitive skin. "Lube. Duh."

He held his pants up with one hand and waddled over to the kitchen table to dig through the gift basket. He found a bottle of lube specifically "formulated for anal sex."

"Super." His face flushed when he thought about Camden selecting that for him.

He didn't want to get lube on the couch, of course, so he shuffled into his bedroom and sat on his bed, his back against the headboard.

Then he scooted down so his head was on his pillow.

That was better. He could almost pretend he was lying down for an evening nap.

He shucked his pants and underwear to midthigh. Taking off his cardigan was probably a smart idea, so he did that too, leaving behind nothing but his T-shirt. Lastly, he removed his glasses. He hated how they slipped down his nose when he got sweaty.

Okay. A squirt of lube, and he would be rocking and rolling.

Time to get the show on the road.

A long, winding road ... full of briars ... and potholes ... and black ice.

Too bad his body wasn't cooperating anymore. His erection was gone.

It wasn't that Theo didn't want to try the Fleshstroker. *He did.* He thought he'd enjoy it, and it would be novel to get off with something other than his left hand for once. But his brain was tripping him up.

He pulled up porn on his phone, but after a few minutes, he knew it was a lost cause. He was worried his neighbor with the shih tzu could hear the artificial moaning.

So, instead, he imagined having sex with Hawke.

No luck.

He didn't know enough about Hawke—other than his body-piercing situation and that he was a sex-toy aficionado—to get his imagination revving.

Guiltily, Theo let his brain run through a turnstile of hot couples that he had basically written fanfiction about in his head through the years. A part-time barista from Bold Brew named Levi and his big, hot boyfriend, Joe. The queer couple from *Schitt's Creek*. Camden and the gorgeous woman he'd made out with on the dancefloor of a gay bar on New Year's Eve six years ago.

Theo focused on his breathing, realizing his heart was pounding and not in a good way. This wasn't working, and he wanted this to work *so badly*. He wanted to be adventurous for once in his entire freaking life, but maybe he needed to deal with the fact that, regardless of his wishes, it wasn't realistic for him. Maybe he was too stuffy to get down with sex toys. Which meant he'd have little chance with Hawke Howard. Or, potentially, most people. Practically everyone used sex toys now, right? They were mainstream like tattoos and craft beer.

He snapped up his phone and called Camden. Without waiting for Camden to say anything, he babbled, "It's not working. I can't do this. You should return the sex toys I haven't opened. I don't need to date Hawke Howard. I mean, going to my ex's wedding by myself isn't the end of the world, and if worse comes to worst, I'll go with you like you suggested." A long silence filled the line between them, so Theo cleared his throat. "Uh. Sorry. Hi, Cam. Are you busy?"

When Camden answered, his voice was all scratchy. "No. I'm not busy. What's the problem? What's not working?"

"I'm trying to use the Fleshstroker, but I can't turn my brain off enough to ... well, you know."

"Maybe the Fleshstroker isn't the toy for you. And that's okay."

Theo pressed two fingers into the opening of the toy, the lube he'd squeezed in there making everything slippery. He shuddered, and a pulse of heat hit him in the stomach. "I'm not sure that's it."

"You don't have to do anything you don't want to do, including play with the sex toys I bought you. But you're welcome to them, even if you don't date Hawke. They're there to make you feel good, and they're in your control. It's just you and that toy, hon."

Camden's voice seemed extra deep on the phone tonight, like he was whispering directly into Theo's ear. A shiver racked Theo's body. He was finally chubbing back up.

"You called me *hon*." That was new.

"Oh ... Sorry."

"It's okay. Was nice." Theo felt winded, and too warm, and oddly disoriented.

"Yeah?"

"Yes."

Camden rumbled in agreement, and that rumble lit Theo up. He squeezed his eyes shut. Camden always made him feel relaxed and safe. They'd known each other for twenty-three years.

"You okay?" Camden asked.

"Uh-huh. But I need ... I don't know what I'm ... Cam, what should I do?"

Another long silence followed those words before Camden said, "Are you hard?"

"Yes." Camden's voice had worked wonders, a fact Theo wasn't going to think too hard about.

"Did you put lube in the Fleshstroker?"

"Yuh-huh."

"Well then, put the opening of the toy on the top of your cock and slide it down."

Theo's brain record scratched. "This is weird, right? We're being weird."

"Why is it weird?"

"Because you're *you*. And I'm *me*. And we're best friends. And I need help, but—"

"I can help you, Theo. Just pretend it's not me on the phone. I can be someone else for ten minutes."

"Oh my God, how am I supposed to pretend it's not you?"

"Umm. How about this?" Camden sucked in a long breath and let it out slowly, the sound reverberating through the line. When he spoke, his voice was even deeper and sultrier. It went straight to Theo's dick. That was, until the words registered. "Thank you for calling Fantasy Sex Phone Line Incorporated. What can I do for you, stud?"

To be fair, the words went to Theo's dick too, after he laughed.

"Stop laughing. You want to come, Theo?" Camden snapped.

"Of course."

"Then put your cock in that little hole right now," Camden growled, his voice mad and domineering, which pinged all kinds of confusing feel-good sensors in Theo's brain.

"Okay, bossy," Theo yelped. He shoved his dick into the Fleshstroker and barely managed to stifle a gratified groan.

"Sounds like the bossiness worked. That what you need? A boss?"

"Uh-huh." Stars were bursting behind Theo's eyelids as he moved the toy over his dick. It was wet and warm and tight in there. He twisted the Fleshstroker when only his head was encased, and a shot of adrenaline pumped through him.

"You better come quickly, Mr. Punch. You need to get back to work. You're way behind on this dataset, and you don't want to disappoint me."

"Oh my God." Theo threw his head back and fucked into the toy, lifting his hips off the bed. No one knew that Theo thought his grumpy boss, Mr. Sauveterre, was a total fox ... No one except for the man on the other end of this phone line. "Y-y-yes, Mr. Sauveterre."

"And do a good job, because if you don't, I *will* make you do it over."

"Okay ... Fuck." Theo peeked down. He moved the toy faster, his dick disappearing into the heavenly sleeve again and again.

"You watch that dirty mouth with me, Theodore." Each word was bitten off and mean, a true scolding coming from a voice that sounded almost alien to him but was also so familiar and dear.

Theo's balls drew up. He tried to hide his shocked moan, but he definitely failed. A burst of sensation flooded his dick, and he came inside his newest, most prized possession.

Once his ears stopped ringing, he stared up at his ceiling fan. Awkwardness threatened to choke him, but he felt too marvelous to let it. They had undoubtedly crossed a line somewhere along the way, like when Camden had pretended to be a phone-sex operator, which was obviously a job Camden would be *amazing* at. Or maybe they'd crossed the line when Camden had imitated *Theo's boss*.

There was a line. And they'd perhaps … tripped it.

"So maybe sex toys are nice after all," Theo said brightly and breathlessly.

Camden's laugh was gruff and deep and shaky. "Yeah. And you've only touched the tip of the iceberg, Mr. Punch."

Even though they were through with the, uh, role-play schtick, Camden calling him Mr. Punch sent a startling, albeit pleasing, prickle over his shoulders.

To distract himself, Theo carefully pulled the Fleshstroker off his cock. He needed to clean it, which, according to the helpful literature, was pretty easy. But it required an end to this conversation.

"I should probably go?" Theo said, his voice rising at

the end as if he'd asked a question. He honestly had no idea how to navigate this situation. What did one do when one got off to one's best friend pretending to be one's bossy boss man over the phone? And why in the goddamn world was he referring to himself as "one" now?

Yikes.

"Are you okay?" Camden asked. He still sounded strange, like a frog was stuck in his throat.

Camden wasn't the one who should sound strange. He was the steady one, the solid one between them. At least when it came to sex stuff.

"Of course."

"And *we're* okay?"

"Yeah. Why wouldn't we be?" Theo said, then scrunched up his nose. He was very aware they might have royally fucked everything up. But it wasn't like Camden was sexually interested in Theo—that would be preposterous—so surely this was fine. Merely a small blip on the large and expansive radar of their friendship.

No biggie.

"No reason, Theo. I'll let you go," Camden said gently. He coughed. "If you need, umm, *help* again, just call me."

Camden hung up before Theo's brain had fully recovered from those words. Maybe this was more than a small blip. Maybe it could be a handful of blips. At least enough blips for Theo to figure out his way around that gift basket. Until he could go on a date with Hawke with confidence.

While Camden had been spilling dirty commands in his ear, Theo's mind had been as close to a pleasurable blank slate as he'd ever experienced, and he didn't want to let go of that yet.

So what if they simply kept doing *this*? Theo would call with each new sex toy he pulled out of the basket, and Camden would pretend to be some amazing fantasy man, and then, in person, they'd act how they always acted.

It was not the worst arrangement in the world.

In fact, it was a pretty tempting one.

CHAPTER SIX

CAMDEN GAPED at his sink of dirty dishes in a daze. Those were not getting done tonight.

He sat down heavily on the floor, leaning his back against his refrigerator. His cock was screaming for attention, but he ignored it. He wanted to really savor the memory of Theo's sharp gasps and harsh breathing. The way his voice went thready and strained the closer he'd gotten to orgasm. Camden had to imprint those moments into his memory now, and if he touched himself, they'd be muddled by the hunger coursing through him.

He didn't know how long he sat on his kitchen floor. Long enough to burn the pizza pockets in the oven to hard, black coals, which sucked because he hated wasting money.

It was impossible to process what had just happened.

He was excited and scared and confused. Mostly, he was terrified he'd fucked up in some huge and immutable way.

But hours later, when Theo sent a text message at midnight asking him, *Did we fuck up?* Camden replied, *We're fine. Pick a new toy to try tomorrow and let me know if you need help. No pressure though. You've probably got the hang of it now.*

Then Camden texted his sister, who was in God knows what country, *I super fucked up. Wish you were here to smack me like when we were kids.*

She didn't answer until the next morning—*More context before the violence, please*—but Camden was already knee deep in bags of salt for the campus walkways and couldn't respond.

He'd had to wake up early because Laurelsburg had gotten a few inches of snow in the middle of the night, and the groundskeeping crew needed to have parking lots and sidewalks cleared before the earliest morning classes.

The hard work and heavy lifting kept him occupied and distracted for most of the day, but as three o'clock rolled around and his shift wrapped up, he was assaulted by the fears—and betrayingly, the hope—from the night before.

He decided to go for a run, donning his winter running shoes and all the necessary layers. He took off from his shitty apartment near campus and let his feet guide him. He passed bars and antique stores and music studios and restaurants. The streets of Laurelsburg had charm, regardless of the season, but he was in love with the city in the winter. It was quieter, stiller. There was a welcoming warmth during the colder time of year that made it feel homey. That was why he'd never left after dropping out of college. He'd been a failure at school—too much partying and missing class—but he'd known Laurelsburg was *it* for him.

Laurelsburg and Theodore Punch—the only things he'd ever been truly sure of.

His mind began to clear of everything but the sound of his studded shoes hitting the ground and the cold burn in his lungs as he ran a maze of downtown side streets.

When he finally took stock of his surroundings, he realized he was only fifty yards from Bold Brew. His feet had led him straight to Theo.

Typical.

Rather than fight it, he moved like a zombie toward the door. He stomped the snow off his shoes as he slipped inside. Theo was at his usual table, but rather than being laser focused on his computer screen, he was staring toward the fireplace, zoned out.

Camden went through the motions of getting a smoothie and a protein bar at the register, but Theo didn't seem to notice him until Camden was right in front of him and speaking.

He said, "Working hard? Don't want to make the real Mr. Sauveterre angry."

Theo startled but sent Camden an automatic smile, which quickly morphed into shyness and embarrassment, perhaps because Camden had not so subtly referenced their phone sex.

Oh, God. Had Camden had *phone sex* with Theo? He hadn't thought of it in so many words until that very moment, and his brain was having trouble deciding if it wanted to electric slide or detonate.

"Hey, Cam. You're wearing tights."

Camden ignored Theo's comment about his wool-lined running leggings and sat down opposite him. Theo always seemed flabbergasted by Camden's workout attire.

"I went for a jog after work and ended up here with you. You okay? You haven't looked away from that fire since I walked in the door."

"I've been distracted today. All week, really." Theo's cheeks turned pink, then pinker, as those words fell between them.

"Yeah." Camden didn't know what to say or do to ease this situation. And maybe Theo's distraction wasn't about him and their role play. Maybe it was about Freddie's wedding. Or a work disagreement. Or Hawke Howard. "Are you hungry? Need a snack? I'll get it for you. Maybe a little food will help with focus. Something nutritious."

Overcompensation for the win.

Theo wrinkled his nose at the word *nutritious*. "A cinnamon roll?"

"Sure."

"With frosting."

"Of course."

Camden stood and went to ruffle Theo's hair, but Theo closed his eyes and leaned in, which threw Camden for such a loop that the hair ruffle turned into a caress. And holy shit, Camden needed to take a good five steps away before he touched Theo again and even more gently.

When Camden returned to the table, plated cinnamon roll in hand, Theo seemed comfortable. He was drinking Camden's smoothie and his laptop screen was filled with spreadsheets and charts and all kinds of stuff that made Camden's head spin.

Theo inhaled the cinnamon roll, and they shared the smoothie back and forth between them.

"You need electrolytes," Theo said. "Did you know the body requires more liquid to stay hydrated in the winter than the summer?"

"I didn't know that." Camden smiled. Things were starting to feel normal between them again, the elephant in the room no longer sitting on his chest.

"I'm going to get you a drink. My treat, since you bought me a cinnamon roll."

Before Camden could blink, Theo was out of his seat and at the register. He returned with a bottle of water, a packet of electrolyte powder, and a matcha tea for himself. Theo prepared the bottle of water with the electrolyte powder for Camden.

"Drink that before you leave." Theo thrust the drink at Camden. "I don't want you to keel over."

Camden dutifully finished half the bottle while Theo chattered away about his new mental-health database project. Once Camden was sure Theo was fine and would be able to get some work done, he jogged home.

He went about his evening routine and convinced himself the whole role-play-until-Theo-orgasmed thing from the night before had been nothing but an apparition. A passing fancy that would never be repeated. He made himself a sandwich and sat in front of the TV to watch basketball.

As halftime rolled around, his early morning caught up with him, and he started to doze. When his phone rang, he didn't open his eyes to answer it.

"Hello?"

There was a beat of silence. Camden's heartbeat skipped, and he sat up.

He knew who it was, and the person calling hadn't even spoken yet.

"It's me. Again."

CHAPTER SEVEN

"HI, THEO," Camden said. He felt groggy, like this was a dream. The best dream.

"Hey. Is it okay that I called?" Theo asked.

"Of course."

Camden clicked off the TV, leaving the living room dark. Arousal spiraled through him, making his blood pump and nerve endings wake up.

"I'm staring at the pile of ... well, you know. The gifts you got me."

"All right."

"I tried to distract myself tonight, by the way. Tried to watch Netflix. Played videogames. Read the same paragraph in a book for an hour. I couldn't stop ..."

"Stop what?" Camden asked, feeling winded already.

"Wanting to experiment." Theo grumbled inaudibly,

and Camden could picture him grabbing his own hair. He'd seen Theo do that so many times in the past when he was amped up or anxious. "You didn't tell me what toy to try, so I have no idea. And there are so many. It's overwhelming. Like what's better—a butt plug or a dildo? Oh my God, I can't believe I just asked you that. What the fuckity fuck am I doing?"

Camden jumped to his feet as if he could stop Theo from hanging up by physically moving quickly. "Hey, whoa. It's okay. Deep breath. I'll help you choose. How about that?"

"Are you going to pretend to be my boss while doing it?"

Camden couldn't tell if that appealed to Theo tonight or not. The question felt like a minefield. "Not unless you want me to. I was going to be myself for a bit."

"I don't want you to be Mr. Sauveterre tonight."

"Okay. Then I won't be." Camden paced to his front window and back to his sofa. Three steps one way. Three steps back. "Find the box that says Rimmy, the box with the purple dildo, and the box that says Supreme P-Spot Pulse."

He could hear Theo shuffling around. After about a minute, he said, "Okay. Done. Do I use all these at once?"

Camden laughed. He was so in love with the man. "No. Not all at once. One of those will be great if you ... well ... if you want something inside you. I should have asked you that first. I was going to have you gather several items and go from there."

"Something inside sounds good."

"Okay." Dizziness almost brought Camden to his knees. "Great. Uh, well, it depends on what you want, then. The Rimmy is a butt plug that has little rotating beads around the neck. It simulates the sensation of being rimmed. You'd need to charge that for an hour or so before use. The dildo is pretty self-explanatory. It's got a suction cup, so you could stick it to stuff, like a shower wall or a headboard. And the Supreme P-Spot is a simple prostate massager. It requires batteries, but I put some in the basket."

Theo didn't respond.

Camden checked his phone screen, but the call hadn't dropped. "Theodore?"

"Yup. Still here. Just trying not to combust from the—"

"Weirdness?" Camden asked, insecurities clawing at his chest. He was trying to treat Theo like he was any other patron at First-Rate, but it was hard to ignore that this was a new step in their friendship.

"I was gonna say hotness, but weirdness works."

Hotness.

Holy shit.

Theo thought Camden's customer-service spiel was hot?

"I'm glad."

"About what?"

"That you think it's hot." Camden rested his flaming face against the cool glass of his window. "So, what'll it be? Plug, dildo, or prostate massager?"

"Hmm. I'd like to try the Rimmy. Do you mind waiting for an hour while it charges?"

Camden fumbled his phone. Theo wanted him to be ... *involved* again? "I can wait."

"Cool. I'll call you back."

"Okay. Don't forget to wash it first." *Jesus.* Wash it first? When had Camden's game completely abandoned him?

"Got it. Bye."

Camden circled his shoebox-sized living room, wishing, not for the first time, that he had more real estate to move around in. He could hear his next-door neighbors, a group of college girls, playing *Call of Duty* and shouting over the game at each other. He glanced out his front window to see a herd of twentysomethings by the pool, which was closed for winter. They had a keg tapped. He couldn't wait to get out of there, but it was the only place he could easily afford without getting a roommate.

He checked his watch, thinking it had surely been close to an hour, but only ten minutes had passed. He decided to take a shower. It was very tempting to jerk off. He hadn't touched himself at all the first time Theo had *needed help*. It would have felt like a violation of trust.

Of course, Camden had jerked off to thoughts of Theo in the past. The way Theo groaned when he ate any kind of baked good. Or how his eyes got hazy and heavy when he'd been drinking—an expression that too closely mimicked what Camden imagined to be Theodore's sexually satisfied face.

But there was something very different about pleasuring himself with Theodore on the phone, especially when that hadn't been agreed upon. He worried it would be a step too far and didn't want to betray Theo's trust.

He turned the water off. He was scared he'd miss Theo's phone call if he took too long, so no quick shower orgasm for him.

He was painfully, achingly hard, but he would ignore it. Ignoring his feelings for Theo in order to function was something he was very accomplished at, and he had never been accomplished at much, so he was pretty proud of himself about it.

He would figure out how to ignore this too.

Once he was out of the shower, he threw on a pair of sweats and starfished in the middle of his bed, prepared to wait for Theo's call. Luckily, it came within two minutes.

Camden scrambled for his phone, then waited for it to ring one more time so he didn't seem desperate.

"Hello." No answer. "Theo?"

"Hey. I'm here."

"You okay?" All Camden wanted was for Theo to be

okay. To be happy and healthy and content. Camden's own desires and dreams were immaterial.

"I'm ... No. I'm not sure how to start."

"There's a remote that turns it on."

Theo sighed, and it sounded like annoyance, which made Camden abnormally happy. He knew that sigh. He loved that sigh.

"I read the instruction booklet. I meant ... Do I just shove this thing up there and wait for it to feel good? That seems clinical."

Camden wanted to explain that it would most certainly feel good, but of course, he didn't know that for a fact. He loved the Rimmy. He owned several, in fact, but everyone's body was different. It might do nothing for Theo. Or it could be irritating or uncomfortable.

So he wasn't sure how Theo should start either. The Rimmy wasn't a huge plug, but it wasn't exactly tiny. If Camden were using it, he'd have to stretch himself.

"Well, that depends on you, and what you need in order to get the plug inside. Some people might want a bit of prep, but others are able—"

"*Cam.*"

Camden closed his eyes and shivered. He loved when Theo shortened his name. "Yeah?"

"I, umm, don't need a WikiHow, exactly."

"Okay. What do you need?"

A long silence followed, but Camden didn't rush to fill

it. It was full of potential. The silences were like poetry, stuffed with meaning Camden didn't understand. He had failed his literature classes, after all.

"I don't know," Theo finally whispered, his voice pained. "A way to relax and ... get on with it?"

If this were a seduction, Camden knew what he'd say. He'd sweet talk Theo into understanding that it was freeing to give yourself pleasure without anyone else's demands in your head, to focus only on what *you* desired. That jerking off, particularly with a toy as decadent as the Rimmy, was worth enjoying. Worth reveling in.

It was definitely worth more than just *getting on with.*

"I think you'll like it, Theo," he said, his voice scratchy. "Last time I played with the Rimmy, it was ... Well, you probably don't want the details, but it's—"

"No. Give me the details."

"Really?"

"Yeah. Please."

"Uh, all right. I was seeing this guy named Raj," Camden said. *Seeing* was a misnomer, except for the fact that Raj *saw* Camden without his pants on twice. Camden didn't try to date anymore, hadn't in a long time, but every once in a while, the loneliness got to him. Raj had wanted fun, casual, and short, which had been great.

"Keep going. Set the scene. I'm going to imagine I'm you."

Damn. Theo kept blowing Camden's mind without even trying.

"We were at his place, and he had this amazing leather couch. It was Christmastime, so he had a tree up, and that was the only light in the room."

"This was recent, then?" Theo asked, his voice soft. Christmas was only a few weeks behind them.

"Oh, no. Over a year ago."

"Gotcha. Keep going. Get to the interesting part."

Camden laughed. "Now who's bossy."

"*Me.* Tell me what happened next."

"Okay, okay. He took my clothes off and laid me down on his fancy sofa. Are your clothes off, Theo?"

"Yes."

"Good. Then he fingered me, nice and slow." A small, hitching moan floated over the line, and Camden smiled. "You stretching yourself? You have to get yourself ready for the toy. It's wide."

"Uh-huh."

Camden held in a horny grunt and pressed his palm to his aching dick. This was torture, but he didn't want it to end.

Camden decided to change tack slightly, to craft a fantasy for his best friend. "He's excellent at finger-fucking you, hitting that hot spot inside you hard over and over again. Until you're begging for it."

"*Ah ... ah ...* oh God."

"That's it. Until you're begging, Theo."

There was a real moan this time, not stifled at all, and Camden about shot through the roof. His whole body clenched, and he had to rip his hand away from his pants.

"Please. *Fuck* ... please, tell me what to do next," Theo gasped out.

"Put some lube on the toy. Make sure to put it around the neck too."

A few seconds later, Theo said, "Done."

"Now he works it inside you. It takes a few minutes because it's been a while, and you don't do this with other people very often." Heat rushed through Camden. He was sliding into the realm of personal information about himself rather than dirty talk, but Theo's noises indicated he wasn't tripped up—much the opposite—so Camden carried on. "Once it's in your ass, he licks your balls into his mouth as he lets you get used to it. Play with your balls, Theo."

"I like that," Theo said. He sounded sex drunk.

"You like what?" Camden asked, mostly because he couldn't help himself.

"Touching my nuts. Having someone else touch them ... or lick them."

"Mmmm. Don't stop, then. Don't stop touching yourself, but press the button on the remote."

Camden waited. He heard Theo whine, deep in his chest, as if something had wrenched inside him.

Camden sat up, his heart rebounding in his throat. "Are you okay?"

"So *good* ... Holy ... Oh my God."

"Feels like being rimmed, doesn't it?"

Theo's response was a gut-punched groan. Camden grinned and pumped his fist in the air.

"What next?" Theo managed after a few minutes of nothing but the sexiest noises on the planet.

Camden fell back on the bed with a thump and let his mind briefly drift to that night with Raj.

"Do you have the Fleshstroker within reach?"

"Uh-huh. Still on my bedside table."

"Is it clean?"

"Yes."

"Grab it and put lube in the hole."

"Okay ... What's next?"

"He blows you." Camden bit his lip hard. He had never been so turned on in his life, and he wasn't doing anything but talking. "He sucks on just the head of your cock until you can't stand it any longer."

Another moment of quiet, but this time the silence wasn't poetry Camden never had any hope of understanding. It was the break in the beat of his favorite song, the breath before the singer belts.

"I'm going to come," Theo said, his voice frantic and shocked. "Oh my God."

Camden's own dick pulsed alarmingly. He managed to shuck his sweats down and grip his dick's base painfully hard to avoid an orgasm.

"Yeah, you are, Theo," Camden said, almost viciously. "You're gonna fuck his throat."

The line went nearly silent, like Theo was holding his breath, but Camden could hear the slick smack of the Fleshstroker against Theo's body. Then Theo cried out, and it was so satisfied and triumphant. Camden wanted to see that joy in person, to feel it as it flushed through Theo, to taste it with his own lips.

"Cam, holy fuck. That was—"

The call went dead completely. *Dropped.* Camden stared at his phone, worry and arousal vying for the top spot in his brain. He gingerly let go of the stranglehold on his cock, his hand inadvertently skimming to the tip, jostling his foreskin. And arousal won. He came immediately, and spectacularly, all over himself.

So that ... happened.

"*Shit.*"

His phone buzzed, and he glanced blearily at the text message.

Theo: *Sorry. I didn't mean to hang up. My fingers were covered in lube, and they slipped.*

Camden: *No prob. You good?*

Theo: *Yeah. That was the absolute best.*

Camden sighed. He had no idea what the fuck they were doing, and he was terrified he was ruining everything, but that *had* been the absolute best.

CHAPTER EIGHT

LAST NIGHT, Theo had made a disastrous mess of his sheets. And the carpet by his bed. And his phone.

During what might very well have been the greatest orgasm of his existence, he'd rolled or writhed or something onto the bottle of lube, and the next thing he knew, lube was *everywhere*. His weight had drained the entire tube in one go.

Cleaning copious amounts of high-quality lubricant out of his flannel sheets and new carpet was not how Theo had planned to spend his postorgasm glow, but maybe it had been a good thing. He hadn't been able to freak the hell out about coming with Camden's hot voice in his ear.

Again.

Yesterday, the recollections had hit him at work in fits and bursts, the bustle of Bold Brew as background noise. He'd caught himself staring off toward the fire, replaying one of Cam's turns of phrase or ruminating on the deep growl of his voice.

But mostly Theo ignored the memories. If he thought too much, he'd ruin everything. He'd act needy or strange or demanding, and the last thing he wanted to do was ruin it.

In fact, he really wanted to continue the arrangement. His confidence was growing along with his curiosity. He'd be ready for Hawke Howard in no time.

But first, he had some lube to replace.

His regular bottle of lube from the corner store was also empty—an issue Theo hadn't even been aware of until he'd checked that morning. If he had a more active sex life, he'd have known he was out of lube, but, surprise, surprise, he didn't, experiments with Camden notwithstanding.

And the lube Camden had gifted him had been so nice. Smooth and lush and not at all sticky.

The crushed velvet of lube.

The caviar of lube.

So yeah, he was going to First-Rate Finishes for the first time, and he wasn't telling Camden. Camden had been trying to get him to check out the shop for ages, but Theo's innate stuffiness had prevented him from popping in.

No longer. Theo had experienced fancy lube, and he was never going back.

Camden's Saturday shift didn't start until noon, so he

wouldn't be there. Theo figured he'd stop in quickly, grab the lube, and go. No need to linger and overstimulate himself.

There was only one car in the parking lot. Sex-toy shops probably didn't do banging business during breakfast time, no pun intended.

The bell over the door tinkled pleasantly as he made his way in out of the snow. Theo didn't know what he'd expected First-Rate Finishes to be like—maybe a tad tacky or kitschy—but the inside reminded him of a trendy mercantile. If it weren't for the tasteful display of glass dildos by the entrance, he might have thought he'd walked into the wrong store.

Theo scanned the displays and reclaimed-wood shelves, trying to get his bearings and spot the lube.

The patter of footsteps reached Theo as someone appeared in the doorway behind the counter, and it hadn't hit him that he'd have to interact with whoever was working. And that the person working might be—

"Theodore Punch. It's been a while, man."

Hawke Howard. Oh no.

Oh no!

Theo almost turned tail and ran, but his body was rooted to the spot. He managed what he hoped was a serviceable smile but didn't manage to step farther into the store.

Camden hadn't approached Hawke yet about setting

him up with Theo. Cam had said he'd wait until Theo was ready.

But what did *ready* really mean? Theo was not the best judge.

"Can I help ya find anything?" Hawke asked, a southern accent sneaking in. He leaned on the counter in front of him. His forearms were thick and muscled and covered in swirls of colorful tattoos. Hawke gave a lopsided smile, drawing attention to his lips and lip ring. He wasn't the most conventionally attractive dude in the world, but he had a sexy intensity that made Theo edgy.

"L-lube?" Theo whispered.

Hawke's eyes sparkled as he looked Theo up and down. Then he nodded toward a table no more than two feet from where Theo had planted himself. Theo flushed and took a stilted step forward.

He'd only been around Hawke twice in his life—both times at parties Camden had invited Theo to. Hawke had always been nice. He was gregarious and passionate and uber cool but wasn't the type of person Theo normally gravitated toward. Theo much preferred spending time enveloped in the cozy familiarity Camden gave off than the proverbial flames around Hawke. If Hawke were a fire, then Cam was a warm blanket right out of the dryer.

And why the fuck was Theo comparing the two men?

He found the brand of lube Camden had bought him, but First-Rate didn't have it in the regular size—just travel-size and bulk-size. Embarrassment and anxiety swamped him. He'd already been there longer than he'd planned.

Did buying the huge bottle say something about him, other than that it was cheaper by the ounce, and Theo was a stickler for rocking deals? Did it indicate that he had need for an obscene amount of lube, and was that a bad thing?

He could feel Hawke's eyes on him, making his heart beat harder. But when Theo glanced up, Hawke's eyes *weren't* on him. He was flipping through a magazine, waiting patiently for Theo to finish up. So now Theo was creating fantasy narratives in his head like a little kid.

Cool, cool, cool.

He snatched up the bulk bottle of super-fancy lube and strode to the checkout counter.

Hawke straightened slowly and sent Theo another heart-stopping smile. Theo couldn't even enjoy it.

"Good choice." Hawke rang up the lube and started to wrap it in crisp tissue paper.

Theo didn't know what to say, so he blurted, "Cam bought it for me. Then I ran out."

Hawke studied him. "Did he, now? Cam's got the best taste—lube, beer, and handsome friends." Theo gaped at him, and thankfully, Hawke saved him. "I mean *me*, of course."

"Oh. Did you?"

After a crackling pause, Hawke grinned and said,

"No." He finished bagging Theo's lube in a thick paper bag. He sealed the bag with a gold and green sticker with the First-Rate Finishes logo. "It was nice to see you, Theodore."

"You too," Theo stammered. Then he fled, slipping on the icy sidewalk on the way to his car.

Theo had no idea how he would make it through a date with Hawke if he couldn't even buy lube from the guy. Though, to be fair, a date wouldn't involve the exchange of money for personal lubricant, so maybe Theo would fare better.

One thing was for sure; Theo wasn't ready for the full force of Hawke's charisma and experience quite yet. He needed a bit more time with Ca—

He just needed a bit more time.

CHAPTER NINE

THEO AND CAMDEN were fairly predictable creatures. They had routines Theo set his schedule by.

Drinks together at Bold Brew on Monday afternoons once Camden got off work. And dinner from Theo's favorite Mexican food place and beer from Camden's favorite brewery on Saturday evenings. By the end of the night, they often found themselves in the dive bar down the street from Theo's apartment, playing shuffleboard or darts. Theo sucked at darts, so Camden seemed to make it a point to snag the shuffleboard table if it was available.

Theo could set his watch by these routines.

As seven rolled around on Saturday night and Camden had yet to show, Theo worried they'd upset their habits too much to recover from.

Maybe Camden felt uneasy coming over to Theo's since it was the scene of the crime, so to speak. Maybe

Camden needed a break from Theo after spending so much time on the phone with him that week.

It wasn't like Camden to leave Theo hanging, though. They didn't discuss their Saturday plans, unless one of them was sick of enchiladas and wanted Mario's Pizza instead. The plans just happened. They were understood.

They usually happened at 6:45. It was now a quarter past seven.

Plus, Theo had found winter work gloves that used solar technology to keep the wearer's fingers toasty. He'd seen a forecast indicating that temps were going to drop, and he wanted to give them to Camden before the cold snap.

Theo patrolled the entryway of his apartment, getting more and more agitated. If this was the result of *whatever it was that Camden was helping him with*, then he wanted no part of it. Yes, he was mildly addicted to Camden's gruff voice in his ear and the careful fantasies Camden spun. But he also needed enchiladas, and Camden's smile, and *Camden*.

A knock at his door nearly gave Theo a heart attack. He wrenched the door open too quickly, surely giving away the fact that he'd been standing *right there*. He caught Camden's flinch of surprise.

"Oh, thank God. You came." Theo took one of the food bags out of Camden's arms.

"Of course." Camden smiled the smile Theo loved

most. It was almost a frown, his eyebrows down but his lips tipped up. "I took the Bug tonight so I don't have to Uber home, but it was running behind. I should have texted. I'm sorry"

Theo should have realized Camden had taken the Laurelsburg bus system, affectionately nicknamed the Bug. It was sometimes slow, and Camden used it often. Theo wasn't thinking logically at all.

Camden skirted around him and slipped into the kitchen to set the beers down. He seemed at home in Theo's space, which helped Theo relax, the tension winding out of his spine.

Theo sidled up to him and unloaded the containers of food. They moved around each other seamlessly, a dance they did in his kitchen once a week.

But then Camden stopped dancing his part, his movements halting with one hand wrist deep in Theo's silverware drawer.

Theo stilled too and followed Camden's gaze. He was peering through the kitchen wall cutout that overlooked the dining table.

A dining table that had a basket of unopened sex toys on it.

"I should have put those away before you got here," Theo said faintly. After all his angsting about the changes in their friendship, and he hadn't even hidden the sex toys?

Camden unfroze and straightened. He turned to Theo

with a laugh. "Why? I know what's in that basket. I got it for you."

"True. But ... It's private."

Was it really private, though? So far, Camden had been there, metaphorically speaking, for every toy Theo had played with except for one failed attempt at using a cock ring yesterday afternoon.

Theo grabbed his food off the counter and started toward the living room. They always ate on the couch with the TV on in the background, which was why Theo hadn't thought to clear his table—they wouldn't be using it.

Camden followed him, his own food in his hands. They ate in silence for a few minutes, but Theo needed white noise, some kind of distraction. He reached for his TV remote to click it to a show he didn't care about, like SportsCenter.

Camden's rough, working-man hand stopped him, gripping his wrist lightly. The oddest shiver wavered through Theo, but he pushed it to the dark part of his mind with the sign over the door reading Ignore!

"Are you having fun with the toys I got you?" Camden asked. His brow was still furrowed with concern.

"I think you know I am," Theo said wryly.

The most intriguing blush spread over Camden's cheeks. Theo didn't think he'd ever seen strong, steady Camden blush. Not as an adult, at least.

"I want to make sure you're okay."

"I'm fine." And Theo was, for the most part. A bit of an anxious mess, but that wasn't exactly uncommon for him. A scary realization hit him suddenly. He dropped his fork in his food container. "Are *you* okay?"

"This is about you."

Theo was the most selfish knucklehead. He grabbed Camden's hands. "No secrets between us, right?"

Camden blinked a few times before staring down at their entangled fingers. "Right."

"Are you fine with what's been happening? I've been in my own world, and I hadn't thought about your feelings surrounding it." For example, what the hell was Camden's consolation prize here? He was a nice, helpful guy, but talking Theo through using fancy gadgets in bed was above and beyond a standard favor.

"Yes, Theo." Camden turned his hands over in Theo's so their palms were resting together. "I love helping you."

"But ... are you, like, enjoying it?" Theo asked, flushing hot at the question.

"I just said I am."

"No, you said you like being *obliging*."

Camden laughed. "I did not. Keep your fancy words to yourself."

"It seems unfair that you're 'helping' me feel good but not getting anything out of it yourself."

"I am getting something out of it." Camden's mouth tipped up on one side, giving Theo one of his trademark gentle smiles. He was so fucking good looking Theo could hardly stand him sometimes.

"Is that something orgasms? Because that's what I'm talking about, Cam," Theo said, thoroughly tired of talking in code.

Camden tensed. It would have been imperceptible, if not for the fact that Theo was touching him.

"I mean, it's okay if you're not into it in that way," Theo rushed on. "I think I've been in a fog, maybe. Like, it's been really nice and fun, but I want it to be nice and fun for you also, if you know what I mean. Because otherwise I'm worried I'm taking advantage of you. Holy crap, am I taking advantage of you? That's the last thing—"

"*Theo.* Deep breath." Camden let go of Theo's hands and briefly squeezed the ticklish pressure point above his knees.

"Hey!"

"I came last time."

Surely Theo would have noticed Camden having an orgasm over the phone.

He was actually a little pissed he'd missed it.

"You did?"

"Yes. Pretty much immediately after you hung up on me."

"Oh. Why? I mean—" He shook his head. His body felt unpleasantly warm.

Camden's eyebrow quirked, up and down, very

quickly. That eyebrow arch was practically porn. "Do you think it's not hot as hell listening to you?"

"It is? But you do all the talking."

"Yeah." Camden shrugged. "I like that too. So we're okay?"

"We are. Or, I am."

"Me too." Camden turned back to his food. "There's no pressure. You can keep calling me or asking me questions if you want, but it's up to you. I'll follow your lead."

Theo's brain was *overflowing* with questions. He had a lot of them—some of the toys in that gift basket were inconceivably complicated—but he decided they needed a few hours of normalcy before he asked the most pressing ones.

Camden retrieved the remote and rather than putting it on something silly and easy to ignore, he chose an old season of *Jeopardy.*

Theo loved trivia, and he quickly got wrapped up in the drama of it, shouting the answers he knew and getting way too invested in individual contestants.

"You want another beer?" Camden asked.

"No thanks."

"All right." Camden stood and stretched. "I'll make you tea." He strode into the kitchen without another word, and Theo stared after him.

They had that exact conversation every week. Theo

could have written it into a play, he knew the dialogue so well, but it had never hit him so hard. The tea Camden made him wasn't quite as good as Bold Brew's, but it was still terrific. Because Camden was terrific.

A few minutes later, Camden returned, drinks in hand. He passed the steaming mug full of bright green liquid over to Theo and relaxed on the couch, leaning back into the arm and propping his feet on Theo's coffee table.

It felt comfortable. Routine. Theo gave Camden the gloves, which Camden was adequately impressed by. As he should have been, because they were cool. Then they watched the show together, drinking their drinks and enjoying each other's company. After Theo got excited about knowing a particularly difficult Final Jeopardy question, Camden nudged him with his socked foot. Theo grabbed the foot and squeezed, ready to brag about how smart he was, but when he turned, Camden's eyes were soft and tender and trained on him.

Theo's breath left him in a *whoosh*. That gaze was different, wasn't it? Softer than usual. It was likely the— Theo did the calculus in his head—two beers Camden had had over several hours. But Theo knew for a fact that Camden could put away a lot more alcohol than that without feeling any effect.

So, yeah, it wasn't the beer. The difference was Theo.

He was letting his imagination run wild, seeing things that weren't there.

"Another episode, smarty pants?" Camden asked.

"No." Theo stood and gathered up the detritus of their Mexican food. He stumbled into the kitchen.

Camden followed at a slower pace, his movements loose and prowly. Theo had never noticed how sensual ... Nope. Nuh-uh.

That thought was a no-go zone.

Camden stopped at Theo's kitchen table and idly picked through the toys in the basket. He was studying the toys with what Theo assumed was professional curiosity.

Camden was simply good at his job.

Theo dumped the food containers into the garbage and recycle cans under his sink. Then he turned on some music, hoping it would drown out the action in his brain.

"I feel restless," he said finally.

Camden glanced up at him. "Should we go down to the bar?"

"No." The last thing Theo wanted was to try to function in a crowd. He could hardly function in front of his best friend right now.

"What about dancing?" Camden did a funny shimmy, and Theo laughed. Not many people got to see the goofy side of Camden Ray.

"No. Not unless you want to risk injury. I hate dancing. I need at least twenty empty feet to dance without incident."

"We could smoke?" Camden said.

They hadn't done that in ages. The last time Theo had gotten high, he'd been with Freddie and Camden on the roof of the Laurelsburg University English building after Camden had told them he'd flunked out.

"You have pot with you, Cam?" Theo said, trying and failing to sound cool.

"Nope. You?"

"No."

Camden grinned. "Ah well. Probably not a bad thing. It gets me all hot and bothered."

"Yeah. We wouldn't want that." Theo's joke fell like a lead balloon between them, or maybe it only fell flat in his head. Because he *did* want to see Camden hot and bothered. It was a hypothetical thought that he'd shied away from for, *God*, years, he realized, and now his brain was screaming it at him.

He crossed to where Camden still stood next to the basket of toys and grabbed the box of one that seemed unfathomable. "How does this one work?"

CHAPTER TEN

IN HINDSIGHT, Camden maybe should have stuck to the basics with his gift basket—a dildo, a plug, a masturbation sleeve, and lube. But he'd wanted Theo to have the world and, as a result, had gotten a bit carried away.

"I have pretty good powers of deduction, so I assume this goes in my ass, but I have no idea what direction it's supposed to face." Theo held up the box and pointed. "And what is going on here? Is it a tail?"

"It's not a tail." First-Rate Finishes sold amazing tails, and Camden would be lying if he said he'd never thought about Theo wearing one, but this particular toy was a prostate massager attached to an adjustable lasso cock ring, the two parts connected by a silicone cord. "That's a cock ring."

"Oh. That might have been obvious to me if I'd opened

it." He flipped the box over and scowled at it. "Or read the box."

Camden smiled. "Perhaps."

Theo handed the package to Camden. "I tried one of the cock rings you got me, but it didn't fit."

Camden couldn't remember which cock ring he'd put in the basket. Again, he'd gone overboard.

"Sometimes that happens. People have different bodies, and not every toy is one size fits all."

"I feel like I'm just doing something wrong." Theo breezed into his bedroom with a follow-me gesture and didn't return. After a few seconds, Camden obeyed.

Theo was sitting on the bed contemplating a black silicone ring. Camden tossed the boxed toy on the bed and sat down as well.

"If you don't mind me asking, how was it wrong? Did you put it on after you were hard? Because you're supposed to do it while soft."

Theo didn't respond. His body was tense beside Camden's.

"We don't have to talk about this," Camden said, even though it had been Theo who had brought it up.

Finally, Theo blurted, "I went into First-Rate Finishes this morning. Before your afternoon shift."

"Oh. Okay." Subject change. "Isn't it a cool store?"

Before Camden could ask what Theo had bought,

Theo rushed on. "It is. I wish I'd waited until you were working. Hawke was there. I think he flirted with me."

Camden's heart lurched, but he tried to shake off the jealousy. Theo and Hawke were a perfect match. He *wanted* them to hit it off.

That was the whole fucking plan!

"Well, that's good."

Theo stared like he was trying to suss out some deep dark meaning in Camden's expression, "Yeah. I suppose. Will you please show me how to put this on? I cleaned it thoroughly. Or disinfected it. Whatever you call it." He passed the ring over.

Camden tried to remember what dildos he'd bought for Theo and whether any of them would be decent guinea pigs, but his brain kept snagging on the fact that Theo had made sure to mention that the ring had been disinfected. Which meant ... *what* exactly?

"You want me to show you. By demonstrating." Camden looked at the ring in his hand. "On myself?"

Theo nodded. His eyes seemed guileless behind his glasses, like he was in a classroom waiting for the instructor to give out the study guide.

"Are you certain?"

"Yes. If you are. I'm better at hands-on learning."

Okay, now Camden was super stuck on the teacher/student thing. That was not a role play scenario he'd ever fantasized about, and he had lots of strong opinions about the power imbalance in real life, but playacting wasn't real life.

"You've always been the model student, haven't you?" he asked, testing the waters.

A light blazed in Theo's eyes. "Yes. A total teacher's pet."

Jackpot.

"Go get a kitchen chair."

Camden wanted to give Theo a front-row seat. Theo snapped to it, rushing out of the room and coming back with a wooden chair. He placed it facing the side of the bed and sat in it. Camden took off his socks and jeans quickly. Then he stripped his sweatshirt off so he was in nothing but a Henley and hunter-green briefs.

Theo's gaze lingered on Camden's muscular thighs, which Camden worked quite hard on, so the interest felt good. *Too good.*

He needed to get this demo on the road before he got hard.

"Where's your lube? It's more comfortable if you put a bit around the inside."

Theo ducked his head shyly. "It's under the bed."

Keeping lube under the bed rather than in the drawer of a bedside table was an unusual choice. He bent over and spotted it, but it wasn't the bottle he'd bought Theo. It was the enormous refill bottle they sold at First-Rate. No wonder it wasn't in a drawer. It wouldn't have fit. Theo was bright red, so Camden didn't comment on it.

Instead, he hefted the large bottle and placed it on the bedside table.

"Pay attention, Theodore. There will be a test later."

He slipped his underwear off and sat on the bed, opposite Theo in the chair. He'd dreamed of getting naked in front of Theo for more of his life than he cared to admit. This wasn't exactly how he'd imagined it, but—gift, horse, mouth, and all that.

"Yes, Professor Ray. I want an A-plus." Theo blinked at him, perfecting the moue of an apple polisher.

Camden laughed and shook his head. He put lube on the inside of the ring, stretched it out and slipped it over his cock and under his sac.

"Oh. Balls."

Camden was so distracted by the rush of blood to his dick that he almost didn't clock Theo's muttering.

"Huh?"

"You put it under your balls," Theo said.

"Yes. Most of them you can wear either way, but this one's stretchier. So unless you're massive, it's probably too big if it's only around your penis. I should have chosen a different one for you. This style is trickier."

Theo nodded, his eyes trained on Camden's cock, which jumped as if it enjoyed the spotlight.

"What does it feel like, teach?" Theo grinned up at him.

The silliness was making Camden giddy. He was pleased this encounter didn't feel fraught. There was some underlying awkwardness, but that was to be expected with a new partner.

Not that Theo was a new partner.

He wasn't.

Mostly, Camden felt at ease and happy, like he was hanging out with his best friend, but in a way that also made him want to come his brains out.

"Not that you would know the difference without a before and after, but it makes my dick a little harder and bigger, which can be fun when you're fucking someone. It varies by individual, but cock rings generally make my dick extra-sensitive. And when I come, it'll last longer and be more intense."

"Wow. That sounds ..."

"Like something you'd be interested in?"

"Uh-huh." Theo licked his lips absently. "What's next?"

"Well, Theodore Punch. I think it's time for your practicum."

CHAPTER ELEVEN

"WHAT A DIRTY WORD THAT IS. *PRACTICUM*," Theo teased, sitting up straighter in the wooden chair he'd dragged in from the kitchen.

Light role play in person was different than role play over the phone. He couldn't stop smiling at Camden, so he wasn't being a very good fake student. But it didn't matter. Camden was grinning too.

Regardless of whether Camden was filtered through a phone line or on Theo's bed, his voice was sexy. Scratchy and brusque, even as it explained how to properly and safely put on a cock ring. Theo tried to pay attention to Camden's voice this time, to listen for subtle changes as Camden got turned on. He didn't want to miss those variations and indicators the next time they messed around on the phone.

But really, why would they need a next time on the phone when they could do this in person?

With Camden in the flesh, wearing nothing but a gray Henley and cock ring, which was vivid against the base of his beautiful cock, Theo wanted to stare at him forever.

Camden handed over the box with the funny-shaped prostate massager and the confusing cock ring that Theo now realized fastened like a bolo tie.

"What's step one, Theodore?" Camden asked.

"Uh, opening the box."

"Don't be a smart ass."

Theo smirked and tore open the packaging. The toy was velvety and smooth under his fingertips. The prostate massager came with a battery. He started to insert it, but Camden *tsked*.

"Incorrect."

Theo glanced at him and about combusted. Camden was absent-mindedly touching his foreskin, rolling it back and forth over the flared head of his cock. Theo knew Camden like the back of his own hand, but he hadn't known he was uncut. There was so much else he might get to learn.

"*Mr. Punch*," Camden said, leaning back on one elbow on the bed, showing off his body. "Eyes on your own work."

Heat flitted through Theo's core. "It's hard to think when you look like that."

Camden bit his lip on a smile and nodded at the toy in Theo's hands. "Go wash that."

"Oh. *Duh*." Theo jumped up from the chair and stepped into the en-suite bathroom to quickly clean the new toy. When he rushed back into the bedroom, he caught Camden licking pre-come off his own thumb. Theo wasn't able to hold in a noise of wonder.

Camden's expression went dark and hot, and he patted the bed next to him. "Take your clothes off and come here."

Theo tore off his wool cardigan and T-shirt and ripped down his jeans and underwear. He should probably have been embarrassed about how eager he was acting, but the role play created a bit of a boundary in his brain that made it easier to just react. He could playact as the eager student for a few minutes and be not at all embarrassed that in the real world he was simply plain old eager Theodore Punch.

He sat beside Camden on the side of the bed, and they turned toward each other. Camden's gaze was as visceral as a touch on his skin, covering all of him at once. He'd never, *ever* been looked at like that.

He never imagined seeing Camden like this or being *seen* in return. It poked and prodded at tender places inside him he'd normally rather leave untouched.

Camden straightened Theo's glasses, which had been knocked askew by his rushed undressing. "I want you to be able to see clearly," Camden murmured.

"If I have to be soft to put the cock ring on," Theo said, "that's about to be a big problem." He was already sporting a semi.

"Let's get on with that, then." Camden squirted lube on his fingers and rubbed it quickly around the loop of the cock ring. "That should help it slide on and keep from catching on any of your hair."

"Okay." Theo fiddled with the tightening mechanism, which was essentially a metal sliding bead. "Here goes nothing."

He slipped the loop over the head of his cock. "Does this need to go behind my balls?"

"It's your choice. It can go either way."

Theo felt overwhelmed and awkward so rather than messing around with it any longer, he tightened it at the base.

"Does that feel okay?" Camden whispered.

With Camden half-naked and nearby, it was hard to process anything but his gorgeousness. Theo needed a mental block, so he focused on his cock. The skin of his cock was hot and tingling. His dick seemed veiny and red and so fucking huge!

Theo touched the tip lightly just like Camden had been doing to himself earlier. He hissed and pulled his hand away. It was almost too sensitive, but in a way that blew the top off his head.

"Yeah, feels ... God, it feels great."

"We can loosen it if it's too tight."

"No. I'm fine." Theo *was* fine except for the thrill at hearing Camden say the word *we*, as if Camden would help if Theo needed it. That appealed to Theo way too much.

"As your instructor, it's important to tell you that you shouldn't wear a cock ring for very long. Recommendation is no longer than thirty minutes at a time."

"Yes, professor," Theo said with a laugh, his voice breathless.

Camden joined in his laughter, and Theo couldn't resist scooting closer. He tilted his head until it rested against the crest of Camden's shoulder. It felt so good—so comforting—to *touch*.

They were not strangers to touching. Camden often rumpled Theo's hair or gave him hugs. That attention usually lit Theo from the inside out, made him amped and happy.

This touch, as simple as his cheek against Camden's clothed shoulder, was altogether different. He felt like his insides were melting together, making him pliable.

"Now for all the marbles. Or all the A-pluses, I guess. What do you do with this?" Camden tapped his fingertip to the prostate massager that Theo had laying across his lap. It was attached to the cock ring via a cord that was the same type of silicone as the ring. Theo had been ignoring it.

"I ... uh ... Well, I guess I shove it in and turn it on."

"*Hmm.* B-minus answer, at best."

"Oh. What's the correct response, professor?" Theo asked. "I hate getting answers wrong."

Camden nudged their temples together in a way that was so affectionate it made Theo's stomach tumble. "You lie back and enjoy it." With a small push to Theo's shoulder, Camden sent him sinking onto his back.

Theo blinked up at the ceiling in surprise. Then, suddenly, Camden was braced above him, smiling down. Theo's senses were full of Camden's spruce-scented soap and sweet-smelling aftershave. Theo wanted to lick his stubbly cheek.

"You ready to have your mind blown, Theodore?"

"Y-yes. I think so."

"Remember, if you don't like it, we stop. You're in charge."

"Do you like it? Using this toy on yourself?" Theo asked.

"I don't have this exact one, but I enjoy the individual components here and thought you might too." Camden held up the lube. "On your fingers or directly on the toy?"

Theo lifted his fingers. He typically finger-fucked himself as prep, but it made him nervous that Camden would witness it firsthand.

To distract himself from Camden's intensity, Theo

gasped out, "What do you like about using a prostate massager?"

Theo circled his hole with wet fingers, lighting up the nerves there. It didn't compare to being rimmed. Or the Rimmy, for that matter. But definitely the next best thing. His cock ached and a bead of pre-come rolled down his shaft.

Camden plopped down next to Theo but held himself up on his elbow. "It makes me feel out of control, and sometimes I need that."

Damn, an out-of-control Camden would be a sight to behold. And a huge turn-on. Theo pressed his fingers inside, sucking in a heady, hiccupping breath.

"That's so hot, Theo."

"I want to feel out of control, like you said," he rasped. He was scared, though. Scared the sensation would be too much in a bad way. Scared it would be amazing, and he'd embarrass himself by making a weird noise. Scared the experience would rip open his chest and leave him vulnerable and exposed.

"Here." Camden doused the massager in lube. Every miniscule movement of the toy caused a tug on the cock ring, keeping Theo needy and on the edge of being overcome. "This button on the bottom turns it on. This part rests against your perineum." He handed it over.

Nervous laughter hit Theo, and he had to bite it back. "What, no exam question? Are you done being my professor?" Theo closed his eyes and bent his knees. It was easier to do this without being able to see Camden watching him.

He felt Camden's rumbly laugh, though. Felt it through his entire body.

"All right. First extra-credit question. What's another word for perineum?"

Theo smiled and pressed the toy inside his ass. It was an easy enough slide, and he could tell immediately that the shape was specifically crafted so the curved head would rest against his prostate.

"Still okay?" Camden asked.

Theo nodded. The silicone cord connected to the cock ring was nestled against his balls, and his heart seemed to be beating in the head of his cock.

"Turn it on when you're ready."

With his eyes closed, Theo felt disconnected from reality, like Camden was only a voice in the room. That was, until Camden brushed a lock of hair off Theo's forehead, his fingers lingering at Theo's brow.

Theo was slammed back into his body, into the moment. He opened his eyes and pressed the button.

"*Fuck*. Taint." Theo's mouth fell open, and he arched his neck, digging the back of his head into the mattress.

Camden's hand traveled to Theo's cheek, cupping it. "What did you just say?"

"I ... Oh God ... I answered your exam question."

"Oh." Camden chuckled. "Extra credit for you. Ten points."

"Only ten? Should be at least ... *Jesus Christ on a bike,* Camden."

"That's Professor Ray to you."

Theo laughed and rolled closer to Camden so they were facing each other.

The buzz against his prostate was mind-numbingly good. Theo liked to be fucked, but it had never equated to such consistent stimulation, especially since most of his experiences were with strangers or minor acquaintances who didn't exactly take the time to get to know his body.

And then there was Freddie, who, well ... He didn't want to think about Freddie right now. At all.

Theo knew his own body. That was the important thing. He knew instinctively that if he clenched, it would increase the pressure and intensity. He shivered.

"That's it, Theo," Camden whispered.

Theo let his gaze roam over Camden. He loved the way their bodies looked together. His pale skin and lean figure next to Camden's tan skin and jacked muscles. His longer, thinner cock next to Camden's fat, uncut one.

It would be even better if they were pressed close, but he was too scared to move that extra foot and some change. Or, maybe he wasn't desperate enough yet. It was getting close, though.

The vibration against his prostate, combined with the

cock ring, was making his whole lower half throb in anticipation. His balls felt full and achy and his dick hard and almost painfully sensitive. He should jerk off. His body was begging him to do something besides let it hang there in suspended arousal.

But he could also smell Camden's fresh sweat. He could feel the heat from Camden's skin and the brush of his labored breaths. Neither of them moved, but their cocks strained toward each other like magnets trying to find their opposite poles.

Theo whined and writhed a bit closer.

"What do you need, Theo?" Camden whispered, his voice soft and secret, just between them. He'd dropped the flimsy role-play act.

"You feel good," Theo managed through gritted teeth. His arousal was getting dire now. A gossamer thread of pre-come slipped from his tip.

"You're not touching me," Camden said. "How do I feel good?"

They'd already jumped, hopped, and skipped over too many lines to count, and Theo should have been scared to step over another, but he wasn't. His brain was too muddled with endorphins and Camden's perfect scent to think about repercussions.

"You *will* feel good … When I get up the nerve to touch you."

Their eyes met, and they seemed to move as one.

Theo went for a kiss because he suddenly couldn't imagine *not* kissing Camden, but Camden ducked his head and placed his mouth at Theo's throat.

It felt intentional, that dodge. Theo hadn't known he'd wanted the kiss before it was taken away, and yet it gutted him.

But then Camden's hands were scraping down Theo's back, and Theo wrestled Camden out of his Henley. Finally, their chests met. They were completely naked, naked in all the ways. Theo's cockhead rubbed lightly over Camden's shaft. Hurt feelings were momentarily forgotten. Nothing else existed but the wild sensations coursing through him. He grabbed Camden's silky cock and Camden grabbed his.

The first inkling of an orgasm flickered in the base of Theo's spine, but it took forever to bloom into something full-throated. He strained closer and closer to Camden until they were wrapped tight in each other, until he could *feel* Camden's strong thighs and jacked arms and body hair and sweat.

The world blurred around him. Nothing mattered but slowly falling to pieces in the arms of Camden Ray. He shook, his body reaching and reaching for a precipice he didn't fully understand but knew he wanted. Without conscious thought, he lifted his mouth toward Camden's again, and this time Camden didn't reject him. Their lips brushed. Camden gasped like he was in pain and kissed

Theo hard, invading his mouth and his mind. Theo's orgasm wrenched to the surface, and he flew.

It lasted longer than ever before. Theo was still trembling when Camden thrust forcefully into his palm and bit down on the side of his neck. Camden groaned and shot all over Theo's stomach.

Theo tried to breathe, tried to calm the violent pounding of his heart. His orgasm had drained him. He managed to turn the prostate massager off without untangling himself from Camden.

Camden touched Theo's shoulder, then the side of his neck. His hand was slightly sticky, and Theo assumed it was semen, which made his pulse flutter. He'd never been one for messy sex, but with Camden, in this scenario, he liked it.

He'd liked a lot about what had happened.

He'd liked all of it.

Eventually, Camden leaned back. "I'm sorry. We should have talked health and safety before that, even though what we did was incredibly low risk. I was tested about ten months ago. All clear."

Theo's stomach flipped over, and he fought a frown. He was hardly capable of speaking, much less carrying on a complex conversation, and he'd wanted to live in the glossy glow for a bit longer.

To be honest, he resented the abrupt body slam into real-world worries.

"Ten months is a long time. You've been with people since, right?" Theo had no idea why that was what he deemed most pressing, but he felt pretty proud he could string a sentence together. "I was tested at my yearly physical in November, and everything was fine."

Camden rolled farther away and gingerly took his cock ring off. When he was done, he didn't meet Theo's eyes and warning sirens started to go off in Theo's head. A confused knot of fear gathered in his chest. Something bad was happening here, but Theo didn't know what it was.

"I haven't been with anyone in over a year," Camden said gruffly. He shrugged like it was no big deal.

Theo thought it was a very big, very shocking deal. Camden could have gone on any app, to any party, to any bar, snapped his fingers and told people to form a line. In fact, Theo had assumed Camden did that regularly.

Camden said things sometimes that explicitly gave Theo that impression.

"Are you telling me I've had sex more recently than you?" Theo asked.

Camden's eyes flashed. "It's not a competition. Plus, I'm pretty sure we're even, considering we just came more or less simultaneously."

Theo waved that away. "No. This doesn't count."

A long silence followed Theo's words.

"Okay." Camden's face shut down, and Theo cringed.

He was screwing this up. In fact, this was one of his

worst, most awkward postsex conversations ever, and he'd had some doozies. It didn't make sense that it was happening with Camden, who knew him better than anyone.

Or maybe it made all the sense.

He couldn't stop the words from tumbling out of his mouth, though. "So you've been celibate? Why?"

Theo had had dry spells that had lasted over a year, but Camden had always seemed to have infinite partners at his beck and call. If he hadn't been with anyone in over a year, Theo had to assume it was by choice.

Camden blinked and got up on his knees. His expression was pleasant and blank, and Theo would have given anything to get back to that place of fiery intensity between them.

"I'm sorry. That's none of my business," Theo said. The no-secrets portion of the night was evidently over.

"We need to get this off you." Camden gently loosened the lasso on Theo's cock ring, taking an infinite amount of care. Theo's chest ached, sharp and sudden. "I'll let you get the rest," Camden said, gesturing toward Theo's groin to indicate the prostate massager. "And I'll get us both a wet washrag."

Camden climbed off the bed and walked toward Theo's bathroom. As the door closed behind him, Theo was sure he was losing something he might never get back.

CHAPTER TWELVE

CAMDEN'S HANDS shook as he doused a washcloth in warm water. His face felt like it was boiling, and his ears were ringing. He closed his eyes and breathed slowly, in and out.

He didn't know what was happening to him. Or why. Maybe fooling around with Theo had been so earth-shattering that his body was making him feel sick.

Unlikely, but it was a better explanation than the one that was lingering at the edges of his mind. It was better than admitting that he was terrified and embarrassed and so, so angry at himself.

This was not the start of a romance between him and Theo.

That was obvious.

It was a random collision of their bodies. Their mouths.

And fuck! They'd kissed. Theo had tasted of matcha, and Camden wished it had been slower. That the kiss hadn't happened during sex.

The first time Camden had thought about kissing Theo had been at their junior prom. Theo's date, a nice girl on the quiz-bowl team, had abandoned him to hang out with her friends since Theo had refused to set foot on the dancefloor.

Camden's date had been drunk. Camden had also been drunk.

He'd found Theo outside, leaning enticingly against the building and staring up at the stars. His skin had looked silvery, and he'd smiled so wide at Camden. Camden had never seen anything so beautiful.

He would have kissed Theo that day. A combination of drunkenness and teenage lack of self-preservation. He would have kissed Theo, but Freddie had turned the corner and grabbed them both in a headlock, one under each arm, and Theo had laughed so hard he'd snorted. The opportunity had disintegrated in Camden's hands.

That hadn't been the last time Camden had almost kissed Theo, but something ... or *someone* ... had always been between them. Freddie had been between them, even when he wasn't physically there.

Tonight, Camden's brain had felt Freddie-free. Camden's worries about ruining his friendship with Theo had been so far away they might as well have been on another continent.

Until the end.

No. This doesn't count.

Theo's words. Those fucking awful words.

Their intimacy, the heat, the goddamn wonderfulness hadn't counted in Theo's mind.

Theo had said it like it was self-explanatory. *No. This doesn't count.*

Camden needed a reality check. A big one. A Publisher's Clearinghouse-sized reality check.

He'd been able to pretend they weren't at risk of destroying the very best and most important relationship in Camden's life, but pretending wasn't reality.

The truth was that Freddie *was* between them. Theo and Camden were only here, in this postorgasm moment, because Freddie and Theo had fallen in and out of love. Camden was hiding in Theo's bathroom because Theo needed a date for Freddie's wedding. Because Camden had agreed to play matchmaker. Because Camden had let himself get sucked into a fucked-up scheme surrounding sex toys and Hawke Howard. It all started and ended with Freddie.

This really had nothing to do with Camden. He was incidental.

No. This doesn't count.

A knock on the door made him drop the washcloth

onto the tiled floor with a splat.

"Cam, you okay?" Theo asked, his voice painfully hesitant.

Camden swung the door open. They were both still naked, which was ... just great. "I'm fine. You?" He retrieved the washrag and scraped it over the dried come on his stomach.

"Yes. A shower might be better at this point."

"Oh. Okay, sure. Let me get out of your way." Camden felt all turned around. He was usually pretty chill after sex. He prided himself on being laidback and going with the flow. It was easy to be unflappable when emotions weren't on the line. With Theo, his emotions were more than on the line. They were exposed to the elements, waving in the wind.

"We can share." Theo reached over and turned off the faucet, which Camden had left running during his whole internal freak out.

Camden couldn't imagine sharing a shower with Theo in a way that wasn't overtly intimate. He'd want to touch Theo. To look at him. Kiss him again.

But he didn't have that right. He was Theo's sex-toy wilderness guide. He assumed there would be no sex toys in the shower and losing that shield would wreck him. This hadn't meant anything to Theo, and it meant *everything* to Camden.

Everything.

"No thanks." Camden had to clear the lump out of his throat. "I think I'm clean enough."

Theo stared at him, his eyes wide and kind of hurt. He grabbed a towel off a rack and held it not so subtly in front of himself like armor. "Are you going to leave?"

Fuck, Camden was screwing this up. The last thing he wanted was to hurt Theo. "*No.* I'll be here when you get out."

"You promise?"

Theo was standing so close, and he smelled like sex, and Camden's arms reached for him without verifying with his head—or heart—that it was okay.

He managed to keep it from being sensual. Or even romantic. *Mostly.* He wrapped one arm over Theo's shoulder, dragged him close, and smacked a kiss on the side of his head.

"I promise."

While Theo rinsed off, Camden got dressed and sat on the bed. A bed that was rumpled from their extra-curriculars. He jumped up, uncomfortable in Theo's room without him, and spotted the sex toys they'd used. The least he could do was clean the stretchy silicone cock ring. He left the ring and prostate massager combo for Theo to deal with.

He washed the cock ring in Theo's guest bathroom, then waited for him on the couch.

The stillness of the apartment got to him, so he pulled

his phone out to fiddle with it. He was contemplating texting Cassie to ask for advice, when the phone vibrated in his hand. On instinct, he answered, realizing one second too late that it was Freddie. And that it was a video call.

"*Shit.*" Camden glanced toward the bedroom. He could hear the shower running. "Hi, Freddie."

Freddie's face filled the screen, his cream-colored sweater bright against his light brown skin. "Hey, groomsman. What're you up to? You seem all flushed and weird."

"I'm hanging out with Theo."

Freddie seemed taken aback by that. He blinked several times. "Why did you answer, then?"

That was a good fucking question.

"He's in the shower."

A confused silence followed those words. Was it weird for Theo to shower while they were hanging out? It wasn't the first time Camden had been here while Theo showered, but typically it happened because Theo lost track of time and wasn't ready when Camden arrived.

"Are you going out somewhere?"

"Yeah," Camden lied, because that was easier than telling the truth.

"Cool. Speaking of Theo ... He hasn't RSVPed for the wedding. Do you think he'll come? I'm not sure if inviting him was the right call, but we grew up together. I—I suppose I'm being nostalgic."

"He's planning to be there. Put him down for a plus-one also."

"Oh really?" Freddie grinned. "That's exciting. You didn't tell me he was dating anyone."

"I don't gossip about either of you to each other." That was a rule Camden had set very early, and one Theo had respected. Freddie was naturally nosier.

"Because you're no fun. What about you? Are you bringing a date?"

"No. Of course not."

Freddie shook his head. "I worry about you."

"You sound like my sister."

"Your sister is smart, so that's not an insult. For real, though. Aren't you tired of being single?"

Blood rushed to Camden's face. He was tired of being alone, but he only wanted one person. It was pretty hard to conjure love when his heart was already taken. He'd tried in the past, and it hadn't been fair to anyone.

"Not exactly."

Freddie sighed and playfully sang, "*Oh, my heart.* You break it sometimes, Camden. Anyway, I didn't call to blather on about your love life. Or about Theo."

"That's a relief."

"Ha. I love your deadpan, heartless schtick. Reminds me of you in high school. And college. And after college."

Camden couldn't help but laugh. He enjoyed Freddie's biting snark. "It is my best quality."

"Your biceps are your best quality. Anyway, I scheduled a tux-fitting for next week. Think you can make it on Friday evening? If not, you can schedule your own at a more convenient time. I know it's a bit of a drive for you."

"Nah, man. I can be there. Send me the info."

"Great. Hey, we should get a drink after the fitting. Just the two of us. We can catch up."

"I'd like that."

"Me too. Okay, I have three other groomsmen to contact before it gets too late. Love you."

Camden smiled. He wished this conversation hadn't happened here and now, but he missed Freddie, and it was good to see him. "Love you too, bud."

"Oh, and think about finding yourself a plus-one. Theo and I will both be married off one day, and you'll be the spinster."

"Ain't nothing wrong with spinsterhood."

Freddie laughed—his big, boisterous one—and hung up.

The shower was thankfully still running. Freddie was right that Theo would eventually find a partner. Theo said he wanted a boyfriend, and he deserved to get what he wanted.

Camden had promised to help him with that. It had been a whirlwind three days of phone sex and role play, but he needed to get his head back in the matchmaking ballgame before he completely obliterated their entire friendship.

A plan had started to solidify in his brain when the shower shut off and Theo reappeared, all damp and rumpled and adorable in a pair of flannel pajama bottoms and a sweatshirt.

Camden patted the seat next to him, and Theo sat down slowly. He seemed wary, which meant Camden needed to do damage control, stat.

"You okay?" Camden asked.

Theo's eyebrows furrowed slightly, but he nodded. "Yes. You?"

"Yeah. I'm fine. Look, if you're still interested in my help, I've got a plan."

"A plan?"

Camden took a deep breath. "We can start casual. Maybe I could invite some friends to Sara B's, that brewpub out by the highway, and go from there. That might make you more comfortable, to meet him in a group. Or, there's munches and demos at Bold Brew. Oh, the wine bar might be nice. That would—"

"*Camden.* What in the world are you talking about?" Theo's frown thinned out his plush lips. Camden dreamed of those lips.

"I think you're ready."

"For what?"

"A date. With Hawke."

CHAPTER THIRTEEN

THEO DIDN'T WANT to be at Sara B's on a Monday night. Mondays were for matcha tea and hearty food at Bold Brew. Mondays were for Camden and Camden alone.

Rather than their usual Monday meetup, Camden had arranged a "casual outing" with his friends from First-Rate Finishes.

Camden's logic, evidently, was that hanging out with Hawke in a group would soften Theo's anxiety enough that a date would go off without a hitch.

Logic sucked.

Theo stared at the façade of Sara B's through his windshield. He'd never been inside. It was off the town's main drag and far enough away from the common campus haunts that Theo figured the clientele would be older. It seemed like a nice place, and he'd perused the awesome beer menu online before leaving his apartment.

Normally, he would have loved coming here. Been excited about it, even with the prospect of hanging out with what Theo imagined to be Camden's wide and wild social circle. But not tonight. Tonight, all he felt was dread.

Maybe it was the weather. It was sleeting, and he would rather have been cozy and warm by a fire at Bold Brew.

Or maybe it was that he was confused about what had happened with Camden. They'd hardly spoken since, nothing besides text messages about logistics for the outing. Theo had thought about calling him last night, about asking Camden to talk him through using a gorgeous glass dildo that looked like a tentacle. He'd had a whole sea-witch fantasy geared up and ready to go.

But Theo couldn't stop thinking about how Camden had refused to shower with him. About how he leapt out of bed to get his distance.

It wasn't fair of Theo to be hurt. They weren't boyfriends. They'd never really discussed the rules or stipulations surrounding the help Camden was giving him, so Theo had no right to have expectations.

But, in the moment, Theo had wanted ... Well, it was terrifying all the things he'd wanted. He had since managed to bin those yearnings like week-old takeout.

They were nothing but a reaction to endorphins and hormones. Compartmentalization for the win.

Any minute now, Theo would leave the safe confines of his car.

He'd walk into that brewpub, flirt a bit with Hawke, set up a date with him, and another date, and another. They'd fall into infatuation, and go to Freddie's wedding together, and it would be perfect.

Theo wouldn't think about Camden once.

The passenger side door opened, and there was Camden in the flesh, a wry smile on his face. It didn't reach his eyes.

So much for not thinking about him.

"What are you doing sitting out here?" Camden asked.

"Just waiting on you." False, but also ... maybe true. Damn it.

"Ready to shake a leg?"

Theo nodded. This would work out. He'd be okay.

An hour and a half later, Theo wasn't sure he was okay. They were posted up at a table in a dark corner of the bar area. He had an Iron City Lager and a pile of fries in front of him.

He should have been in heaven.

He wasn't.

Camden was across the table from him, sitting *between* a married couple—Diana, who worked at First-Rate, and Yan—both of whom seemed to be very familiar with Camden. Suspiciously familiar. And though Theo was not often sexually attracted to women—he could count on one hand the number of times it had happened—there was no mistaking how incredibly hot both of the ladies were.

Camden *was* attracted to women. He dated just as many women as he did other genders. Or at least that had been Theo's impression. Of course, he'd also thought Camden had lots of casual relationships only to find out he'd been basically celibate for over a year. So what did Theo *really* know?

Nothing. He knew *nothing*.

On Theo's right was a shy woman named Brandilynn. She had a tattoo of Sally from *A Nightmare Before Christmas* on her forearm and a tiny pair of handcuffs below her ear. She was evidently First-Rate Finishes' newest hire. Each time Theo got overwhelmed by Hawke's presence on his left, he turned back to Brandilynn's kind smile.

She seemed to understand.

"Tell me about your job, Theo," Hawke said. Hawke focused on people like they were the most important person in the room. But it didn't have anything on the way Camden had looked at Theo after they'd gotten naked.

Which Theo was not going to think about.

"Even the nicest person's eyes glaze over when I talk about bioinformatics." It wasn't as if Theo sold high-dollar fetish gear. Now, that was a job that could perk up a conversation.

Hawke laughed. "I think you underestimate your appeal."

Theo's face went hot, and he glanced at Camden. Camden nodded at him encouragingly, but Yan was touching his arm and leaning over him to speak to her wife, Diana. Theo zeroed in on that contact, a tight feeling in his chest.

He shifted to face Hawke. He could do this. He could flirt.

"Okay, I analyze hot, hot datasets all day, program very sexy statistical models, and optimize sensual specialized databases."

Hawke's mouth tipped up in a grin. He leaned his elbow on the table and turned his body toward Theo like he was advertising to the whole world that Theo had his full attention. "*Oooh*. Tell me more."

"That's about it. The job is remote, so I do my work at Bold Brew most days. I don't like the silence of my apartment."

"I love Bold Brew. Ralph, Jess, and Aries have created a cool space there."

"Yeah, they have." Of the Bold Brew owners, Theo only knew Ralph, who was a natural caretaker. He worked the floor sometimes and was always there with a smile when Theo needed one.

"I used to go to the Tuesday munch every week."

Theo wasn't sure what to say to that. He knew about the Bold Brew munches—the informal social meetups for the local kink community—but what did it mean that Hawke used to attend? Theo had no idea how to broach the topic. What was the etiquette? Did you ask, *Hey, what's your kink?*

Theo was *not* going to do that.

"Interesting. I like their tea."

Hawke grinned and smoldered. He gave pretty good smolder, Theo had to admit.

"It was nice to see you at First-Rate the other day," Hawke said. "Camden talks about you all the time."

Theo looked at Camden. He had his arm over the back of Diana's chair, and she was curled toward him slightly. Brandilynn had been looped into the little lovefest across the table, her attention on Camden as well. His hair was messy like someone had run their fingers through it.

"It was nice to see you too," Theo said stiffly to Hawke.

A cute young man approached Camden, slinging an arm over his chest and giving him a hug from behind. Theo didn't recognize the guy, but he was obviously friends with Camden.

Everyone was friends with Camden. He was so fucking friendly.

A boiling potion of emotions bubbled up inside Theo, the strongest of which was ugly and unexpected.

He downed about half his beer in one go, then tried to focus on Hawke. Hawke was watching him closely, and Theo flushed.

"I'd love to take you out," Hawke said. "Get to know you better."

"Did Camden tell you to ask me out?" That had been the plan from the beginning, but Theo had pictured it going differently. He'd expected Camden to give both Theo and Hawke a time, date, and location to meet. He hadn't expected Hawke to ask him out and pass it off like it was his own idea.

Hawke's eyes flared in surprise, and he glanced at Camden. Theo studiously did not.

"No. Yesterday, he mentioned in passing that you're single and wanting to date more. I figured I'd shoot my shot. Was he supposed to tell me to ask you out?"

Damn, Camden was a great manipulator. He hadn't even had to explicitly do the matchmaking, just a prod and poke here and there to get his way.

"Yes," Theo said through clenched teeth, trying to smile. He didn't have the energy to lie.

"Seems I preempted him, then. Lucky me. Now we can simply leave Camden out of it. How about that?" Hawke gave Theo a conspiratorial grin.

"Yeah, let's."

"How about dinner on Friday?"

"Sure."

They exchanged numbers, and once that was out of the way, Hawke gave Theo's chin a tiny pinch. "Can't wait, cutie."

It was reminiscent of the hair ruffles Camden gave him but not quite as sweet. Theo peeked across the table. The mystery man was still standing behind Camden, leaning over and talking in his ear, but Camden was staring at Theo, his eyes dark and strange.

The man finished speaking, then gave a round of hugs to Diana, Yan, and Camden. Camden pressed a kiss to the guy's cheek, close to his mouth.

Theo did not like that at all.

He put on his very best smile, rested his chin in his hands, and turned to Hawke. "So, tell me about these munches."

CHAPTER FOURTEEN

THE REST of the night was torture. Theo was short of breath, and his mind was a numbing block of anger every time Camden laughed when someone else spoke, each time he touched another person.

Mondays weren't supposed to go this way. That was why Theo was so mad. It was the only reason that made sense.

He was used to having Camden all to himself on Mondays, and Theo resented the change in routine.

To compensate for his roiling emotions, Theo focused his attention and energy on Hawke, who was charming, kind, and hot. It was going well between them, Theo thought. Or would have been, if he'd been able to stop eyeballing Camden.

Because it was a work night, people started to wrap up and leave, one by one, around eight. Camden cajoled and flirted his way through every goodbye, handing out cheek kisses like candy, until the only people left were Hawke, Camden, and Theo.

"I'm turning into a pumpkin, so it's time for me to go," Camden said.

He ruffled Theo's hair, a move that usually delighted Theo, but today filled him with angry resentment. Why would Camden kiss everyone goodbye but him? Give everyone hugs and his come-hither smile except Theo?

"Hey, thanks for planning this. It was great," Hawke said, standing and shaking Camden's hand. Camden didn't kiss Hawke's cheek either. Hawke turned to Theo. "You ready to head out too, or do you want to stay and chat a bit longer?"

Camden took a step backwards like he was going to back out of the conversation once and for all. That made Theo angry too.

Maybe he was just an awful, angry person this evening.

"I should go home," Theo said. At that, Camden shot Theo a very pointed look, as if to say that Theo was blowing it.

Theo didn't care if he was blowing it.

This didn't feel good. Didn't feel fun.

Hawke smiled. "I'll walk you to your car."

Camden suddenly seemed overly preoccupied with his

cellphone, which pissed Theo off too. Theo had no excuse not to walk out into the sleet next to Hawke.

Hawke smelled amazing, and he shared his umbrella with Theo. On a normal day, he'd blow Theo's socks off.

They said goodbye at Theo's Prius, and Hawke kissed him very tentatively on the cheek. "I can't wait until Friday."

"Neither can I."

Theo waited in his car for a few minutes after Hawke walked away. He saw Camden waltz out of Sara B's. He was on the phone, and a smile flashed across his handsome face as he spoke. He jogged to his truck, got in, then pulled out of the parking lot.

Theo slammed a hand down on the steering wheel. He should have been happy. His plan with Camden had worked. Hawke had asked Theo out. Theo didn't feel so out of his element in regard to the sex-toy situation. He was pretty confident he could hold his own at least.

He didn't know what feelings were coursing through him, but happiness wasn't one of them.

Maybe he needed caffeine. Or to eat a meal more substantial than Sriracha fries.

Or maybe he needed to fight, to focus his angry energy into something productive.

He left the parking lot. He wished he could say that he ended up at Camden's apartment complex because his hands and feet had evolved to have a mind of their own.

That they'd taken him there of their own volition. But that wasn't true.

At the stop sign where he could've gone left to his apartment or right to Camden's, he'd turned right.

His anger and discontent led him straight up to Camden's door. Camden hated his apartment, hated living there surrounded by rowdy college students. Theo could count on one hand the number of times he'd been to Camden's place. He knocked loudly three times.

Bang. Bang. Bang.

It took Camden a full minute to open the door. When he did, he was still on the phone and looked feral and furious.

"Cass, I gotta go. Theo's at the door," Camden said into the cell, staring at Theo and letting him get wind-whipped and wet from the sleet. Cassie must have responded because Camden closed his eyes for a long second before hanging up abruptly.

When Camden opened his eyes, Theo almost recoiled. There was so much emotion in them, and he couldn't tell if it was good or bad or scary or wonderful, but Camden grabbed Theo by the front of his shirt and hauled him inside.

With a gentle shove, he pushed Theo toward his bedroom, and Theo stumbled that way gratefully.

"What do you want, Theodore?" Camden growled.

Theo wanted Camden to lay claim to him. He wanted

to be obliterated, to stop feeling so confused. He wanted that flawless blankness that seemed to only happen when Camden's voice was whispering dirty fantasies in his ear.

He wanted a fight. And a fuck. And to fucking finally feel good.

"Strangers."

"What?" Camden asked.

"I want to pretend you're a controlling stranger who tells me what to do, so I don't have to think about anything anymore. That this can just happen without our history and friendship and bullshit between us."

Camden scanned Theo's face. They were both breathing hard.

"Okay, listen to me closely, Theo. You tell me *no* or *stop* at any moment, and we stop. If you say *wait*, I'll stop. Same goes for me. If I say *stop*, we stop."

"Yes. I understand."

"I'm going to get a toy for you. It's never been used. It was an extra the store got, and Haw—and my boss gave it to me. I'm going to wash it while you take your clothes off."

"Okay." Theo whipped his sweater up and over his head while Camden disappeared into the hallway.

He was slower to take off his boots, socks, and pants. When Camden returned—shirtless, thank God—Theo was down to nothing but his underwear.

"Fuck, you're hot," Camden growled.

Theo barely tracked the words. He was too distracted by the large contraption in Camden's arms.

Theo didn't know what to call it. "Dildo" didn't quite do it justice.

"A dildo plaque?" Theo whispered. Camden started to smile, but the expression died on his face as he met Theo's eyes.

Camden placed the whole apparatus on the padded bench at the end of his bed. Theo could tell it was heavy by the way Camden's arms bulged. Theo ran a finger along the stainless-steel cock. The base of the dildo was soldered to a large, flat, steel plate.

"It's the Steel Slat Fuck Pipe. It's your stranger."

"This thing is nuts."

"Yeah. It's ridiculous. I have nowhere to store it and no idea why I agreed to take it. And you, Theo, are gonna fuck it."

Theo nodded. He was dizzy from the heat flushing through him. Camden's voice was deliciously angry. It matched the frustration pulsing in Theo's chest, his stomach, his groin.

Camden pulled a bottle of lube out of his bedside table and thumped it down hard next to the dildo. Then he stalked behind Theo.

Theo shuddered through the rush of arousal he felt having Camden at his back, Camden's breath hot on his neck. Camden tugged Theo's boxers down, not touching skin.

"Get up there next to it." Camden's voice was short and sharp.

Goosebumps bloomed along Theo's arms, raising his hair. He was about to turn and launch himself at his best friend when Camden prowled back to the bed. He shucked off his pants, kept his underwear on, and sat against his headboard, too far away from Theo's greedy hands. Theo crawled up next to the dildo.

They stared at each other, Theo naked and needy and Camden hard and mad.

"Strangers, yes?" Camden asked.

"Yes."

"Fine." Camden inhaled slowly. "My friend and I have had a long, hard workday, and we're on the hunt for a nice, little slut to make it better. That you, sweetheart?"

"You-your friend?"

Camden nodded toward the dildo.

"Oh. Like a threesome?"

A fine and miniscule smile ticked up the edge of Camden's mouth. "Maybe. Get yourself ready for us."

Theo squirted lube into his hand and closed his eyes. It was hard not to see Camden, to think about Camden, with him front and center. At the same time, he wanted to give Camden the best show in the fucking world, to please him and do as he said.

"*Maybe* a threesome?" Theo ghosted his hand over his dick and balls before reaching his hole.

"Yeah. Maybe he'll fuck you, then I'll fuck you. We'll wear you out until you can hardly stand, hardly think straight."

Theo gasped and pressed his fingers inside. It was difficult at this angle but enough to tease and soften the muscles.

"Maybe we'll fuck you at the same time. Get both our dicks up inside you at once."

"Oh my God."

"You like that idea?"

It sounded hot but also *not at all*. That was the great thing about this. He wasn't actually going to be fucked by two cocks at once. It was a fantasy meant to turn him on. He wasn't being seduced by two strangers either, but with his eyes closed and dirty words being hurled at him, it felt like he was.

When Theo didn't answer in any way but a groan, Camden whispered, "Or maybe I'll watch you ride my buddy until you're spent. I like to watch."

"Please, Cam."

"Who the *fuck* is Cam?"

Theo opened his eyes. The lights had been turned off, all except a dusty lamp by the bed. Everything was shady and dark, which he loved. Made this feel even dirtier.

"What's your name, then?" Theo asked.

"None of your fucking business, sweetheart." The words were a seductive taunt that sent Theo's head reeling again. "Put lube on my friend and saddle up."

Theo followed directions, accidentally putting way too much slick on the dildo. Stainless steel didn't absorb the lube in any way, so the two pumps Theo had used made everything a sloppy mess. He glanced at Camden on the other side of the bed. "I'm sorry. I got that everywhere."

"It's okay." Camden was sprawled against the headboard, his legs and arms relaxed. If it weren't for his balled fists and hard cock, Theo would have thought he was unaffected. "We like it messy. *Now* ... sit on that dick."

Theo swallowed hard and swung a leg over the toy so he had one knee and one foot planted on the padded bench outside the steel plate. He lowered himself onto the head. It was cold and so fucking hard. Unyielding, but in a way that excited him.

"Oh fuck."

"That's it. Take your time."

He twitched his hips, working the dick deeper in small increments, sounds spilling from his mouth. Camden watched him raptly. With one last slide, Theo dropped onto both knees and got the cock to hit him in exactly the right place. He cried out.

Camden jumped, as if the noise had startled him. His legs fell open slightly, giving Theo a view of his package, snug and perfect and bulging in his briefs. The muscles of

Camden's arms stood out in stark relief as he gripped the bedding at his hips.

Camden, Camden, Camden.

The room smelled like him, like his spruce-scented deodorant and vanilla aftershave. The cadence of his breath washed over Theo.

Theo was really struggling to pretend Camden was some stranger.

He moved faster, hoping the bump and grind on his prostate would clear his mind, but it was no use. Camden looked too hot lounging in front of him.

"This is hard," Theo said, his voice strained because he was pretty actively fucking the dildo.

"What is?"

"Pretending you're a stranger. You're right in front of me, and I've known you my whole life."

"Close your eyes."

He shook his head. "Not going to work. Need more."

"Okay. Hold on. Stop moving."

That was harder than it sounded. Theo rested with the steel dick inside him. He moaned, craving the push and pull of movement.

"It's okay, hon. One second." Camden scrambled out of bed and dug around the top drawer of his dresser, returning with a satin blindfold. He held it up. "Yes or no?"

"*Yes.*"

Camden circled behind him again, and Theo had no idea why that was so hot, but it was.

Gently, Camden removed Theo's glasses. "I'll keep these safe." Theo nodded.

With a quickness that belied a lot of practice, Camden had the blindfold over Theo's eyes and tied around the back of his head.

"Yes or no?" Camden asked again.

"God yes."

Theo didn't know if it was the blindfold or the fact that Camden was behind him, but it was easier to pretend he wasn't in his friend's bedroom.

He expected to feel Camden move from behind him and return to the bed, but after several long, breathless seconds, Camden stepped closer and put his mouth to Theo's ear.

That alone was enough to make Theo's cock jerk and his balls ache, but then Camden spoke. "Gonna paint you a picture. You're at a seedy club. A place you should never have gone on your own. Two strangers snag your attention and pull you into a back room. They're big and rough and exciting. It's hot back there, and you're sweating." He licked along the side of Theo's neck and hummed. "Are you gonna give them what they want?"

Theo started to melt down. His skin tingled from the lick, tingled all over, in waves down his spine and over his shoulders.

"Yes."

"That's a good little slut."

Hands gripped Theo's hips from behind and moved him, tentatively at first, then hard, helping him peg all the best places inside him, again and again. Theo tipped his head back, and it connected with a firm, sweaty chest. It was glorious. Hot and messy. Lips crashed into his from over his shoulder, and a tongue raided his mouth.

Oh god, Theo wanted so much. Without being able to see and with a fantasy whispered directly in his ear, he could imagine the club. Low red lights. The scent of sweat and alcohol. Sticky floors. Music pounding to the beat of the blood rushing in his ears. He wanted the fantasy. The threesome fantasy. The strangers fantasy.

He grabbed the arm wrapped around his chest and pulled until the stranger, the most precious stranger in the world, had climbed onto the furniture in front of him. It creaked as it took the stranger's weight. Still blindfolded, Theo fumbled until he found the man's underwear, and callused fingers helped get the offending fabric down. Then Theo planted his hands on something soft, like a bed or a club booth. The change in angle made him cry out, and stars sparked behind his eyelids as solid pressure bumped his prostate.

He used his hands to search for the stranger's hot, hot cock. When he found it, he grabbed on and said, "Yes?"

A gruff voice responded, "Yes, fuck yes."

Theo's lips connected with the tip of the cock. He let his tongue dip around the foreskin.

"Oh God." Rough hands threaded into his hair and held him steady. "Can I move? Can I fuck your mouth?"

Theo was typically cautious about allowing someone free rein. He didn't trust easily. Didn't like allowing people that access. It was a vulnerable position. But all reason, all fear fled his brain, leaving nothing behind but a pleasurable fuzzy haze.

He gasped, "Yes," then braced himself against the stranger's thighs. He didn't need to worry. The cock slid into his mouth sweetly, just deep enough to make his heart thunder but not deep enough to choke him. A short thrust here, a long drag there. It was like he was being gifted the dick in his mouth.

He couldn't help but grab his own, to feel it in his hand, rigid and ready. Wet with pre-come. He trembled, on the edge so fast it hurt.

The dick left his mouth. He whined and chased it.

"Shh. Hey, it's okay." Trembling fingers shifted through Theo's hair. "Want to be able to see you come."

Theo sat up again, and his hand flew over his cock. His body was on overload. He pumped his hips, riding the cock inside him, and he only had a few seconds to be terrified about how hard he was about to come. Then it was there, and he practically screamed as he let go, a whipcord of sensation pulsing through him.

He fell forward on a whine, the abnormally hard cock leaving his body. He could hear breathing in front of him, several feet away. With the blindfold on, he crawled forward until he reached an ankle, then a knee and a strong thigh.

He straddled Camden's lap like it was the most natural thing in the world.

CHAPTER FIFTEEN

CAMDEN WAS SHAKING, and sweat dripped down his chest in rivulets. Witnessing Theo come on that steel dildo was honestly the hottest moment of Camden's life. He'd made a mess of the foot of Camden's bed, then fucking crawled through it to reach Camden's lap.

Theo tore his blindfold down until it was loose around his neck. He touched Camden's bottom lip with the tip of his finger. "Fuck me."

Dreams and desires sprinted through Camden's brain. He pushed almost all of them away.

"Will you be too sore?"

"No. I love being fucked after I come." Theo grabbed Camden's dick like he was going to hop right onto it.

"God, hold on. Need a rubber."

Theo blinked a few times as if he was coming out of a daze. Then he leaned over and tore open the drawer of

Camden's bedside table. He came back with a condom and a travel-size lube bottle.

"You own a lot of lube."

"I know." Camden took the condom from Theo's long, beautiful fingers and put it on. "Theo."

"Yeah?"

"Not strangers. Don't want to do this as strangers." The admission felt like ripping his heart open, but it was a hard line for Camden.

"Not strangers. Just you and me."

Their faces were so close Camden could see the flecks of green in Theo's icy blue irises, see the places where his lower lashes clumped together. Camden grabbed Theo's glasses from the bedside table and gingerly put them back on Theo's face.

"Are you sure?" Camden asked. He liked the role play. Hell, he loved it actually, but he couldn't look Theo in the eye and do this as anyone but himself.

"I'm so sure, Cam." Theo poured lube onto the top of Camden's cock and followed it with his body, taking Camden inside him in one long slide.

Camden wrapped his arms around Theo, pressed his hands into Theo's hot skin, and stared up into his eyes. Theo shivered, and his mouth dropped open.

"You're so beautiful," Camden said, his lips skimming Theo's chin. "Does it feel good for you?"

Theo moved slightly, and his hole clenched around

Camden's cock. "Yes. It's nearly ... too much but amazing."
He skimmed his palms over Camden's shoulders and chest.
"Fuck, you're so strong."

Camden grabbed Theo's hips, not to direct him, but to
sense his movements. To experience the shift of muscle
and bone as he rode Camden's cock slowly, the drag and
pull so wonderful Camden could hardly breathe.

He'd been close for a long time. Just watching Theo
work that steel dildo inside had been enough to make
Camden tense, but then touching Theo, blindfolding him,
fuck, feeling Theo's mouth slip over his foreskin—
Camden's body was close to combusting

Their encounter had started so angry. Camden had
liked it that way. He'd wanted Theo to snarl and snap, and
Camden had wanted to return the favor, to drown out the
jealousy blasting through him. It had been sexy and harsh
and a bad idea.

This was still probably a bad idea. Removing a
blindfold did not a good idea make. Nothing had really
changed, had it? Theo had a date with Hawke on Friday.
Camden had heard as much during his not-so-subtle
eavesdropping.

"Cam," Theo said. His eyelids were at half mast,
satisfaction curling the edges of his lips. His face was an
erotic masterpiece, one Camden would hold onto forever.
"Where'd you go?"

"I'm right here."

Camden's worries and insecurities could wait. This might be a bad idea, but Camden wasn't strong enough to dismiss it or push Theo away. He loved him, he wanted him, and for a few minutes at least, Theo wanted him back.

He gripped Theo's hips a little tighter and thrust up gently. Theo threw his head back and moaned. Sweat beaded along Theo's collarbones, and it was too tempting not to taste. Camden licked along that bright line, and Theo's breath hitched, going ragged. Theo started moving faster as Camden bit and nibbled along the bone and up to the tendon of Theo's neck until Theo was slamming his ass onto Camden's dick.

"Theo," he groaned into skin that smelled so fucking sweet. "Gonna come."

"Do it."

The dam inside him broke. Feelings and sensations rushed to the surface and crested in devastating waves. He clung to Theo like he was a life raft, coming inside him and trying not to let his heart float away.

After catching his breath, Camden was finally with it enough to notice the miniscule shifts of Theo in his lap. Theo's cheeks were flushed and rosy, his lips red and parted.

"You okay?" Camden whispered.

Theo rotated his hips slightly and jolted. "Yes. Just, you have a nice dick. Feels good against my ... Well, you know why it feels good."

Camden smiled and slid his fingertips up Theo's ribs. There were so many places he hadn't gotten to touch yet. Theo's dick was half-hard. He ran his thumb along the slit, and Theo shivered.

"Gonna have to move soon. The condom."

Theo nodded. "I know. Tell me when." Another circle of his hips, and his eyes rolled back.

Sometimes Camden was amazed by the human body, how every person was so different. He couldn't handle having anything inside him for very long after he'd come. Too sensitive. But Theo was eating it up, still drowning in pleasure despite the fact that his cock was obviously spent.

Camden tipped Theo onto his side and pulled out once his own cock started to soften. With a quick and practiced snap, Camden had the condom off and tied so it wouldn't leak. Then he pressed his fingers into Theo's hole and zeroed in on his prostate. He was so warm. Theo's eyes flew open, and he flung a leg over Camden's hip.

"Okay?" Camden asked.

"No one's ever ..." Theo shook his head and snuggled closer. "It's nice."

"No one's ever done this for you after sex?"

"No."

"Not even—"

"Shh." Theo smiled. "Stop talking before you ruin it."

That was fair. Bringing Freddie into a conversation

that didn't need to involve him would have definitely ruined it.

Camden rocked his hand gently until Theo stopped twitching with each movement. At last, Theo let out a long, shaky sigh, and Camden pressed his face against the top of Theo's head.

"We should clean up," Camden said into the mop of curls. Theo made a grumbly noise in return. "Don't move. Rest. My friend and I wore you out, just like I promised. I'll get a washrag."

Theo laughed and promptly fell asleep.

CHAPTER SIXTEEN

THE FIRST TIME Theo woke up, it was dark outside, and Camden was sitting up in bed, his back against the headboard, watching the sleet batter the window. He was a picture of pensive handsomeness.

Theo must have made a noise, because Camden looked down at him and said, "Hey, sleepyhead."

"Sorry. Conked out on you." Theo's voice was scratchy, and his eyes felt heavy. "Do I need to go?" he asked. Theo couldn't quite remember why it was a bad idea for him to sleep in Camden's bed, but the reason niggled at the back of his mind.

Camden brushed a hand through Theo's curls. "No. Go back to sleep. It's late."

"You sure?" A wide yawn cracked Theo's jaw.

"Positive." Camden's hand slid to the back of Theo's

neck, and his thumb worked some kind of magic because Theo lost consciousness almost immediately.

The next time Theo woke up, it was morning. Weak, blueish light streamed through the curtains. The night before returned to him in a rush.

His heart hammered in his chest, and he glanced around the room wildly, snatching up his glasses from the bedside table. All evidence of his night with Camden was gone. The ridiculously impressive steel dildo thing. The lube. The condom Camden had tossed on the floor. There wasn't even evidence on Theo's body. No lingering stickiness or dried come.

But Camden was asleep next to him, curled up on his side, his face half on Theo's pillow and half on his own. They'd slept so close to each other. Close enough to touch. Theo was breathless just thinking about it.

Camden's jaw was shadowed with stubble, and one of his hands was fisted next to his cheek. Theo remembered Camden sleeping with his hand up next to his face during their childhood sleepovers. The realization that Camden still slept like that sent a wave of intense tenderness through Theo.

The anger from the night before that had driven him here was nothing but a dull twinge in his stomach, and he felt ... happy? Maybe satisfied was a better word. Happiness was hard to quantify, and, regardless, he wasn't awake enough to tackle his emotions.

It was a Tuesday morning, and they both had to go to work. Theo had no idea what time it was. He slipped out of bed as soundlessly as possible. Camden had folded Theo's clothes into a neat pile on the bench at the end of the bed. The bench that Theo would henceforth refer to as the fuck bench. When he found his jeans, he pulled his phone out to check the time. It wasn't yet seven.

He sat on the fuck bench and tried to remember what time Camden reported for his groundskeeping shifts. On days with horrible overnight snow, he went in as early as five, but Theo had no idea if the sleet from the night before represented such an emergency.

He suspected not, which meant that he had time to ... do what? His feet were pulling him toward the door, but surprisingly, it wasn't to make a secretive escape.

Theo wanted to do something nice for Camden. Last night, Camden had welcomed him in, despite Theo being mad and reckless. Camden had given Theo everything he'd wanted. Everything he'd *needed*. That was Camden to a tee. He was always taking care of Theo. Maybe it was Theo's turn to give some care back.

He assumed Camden hadn't gotten much sleep the night before, if his foggy middle-of-the-night recollection was correct, so he took great pains to sneak out quietly. He locked the door behind him.

It was a quick drive to Bold Brew. The early morning crowd was sparse, and there was no line. Theo took his time selecting a variety of treats—donuts, cinnamon rolls, and muffins—which the barista loaded into a box for him. He also grabbed a few of the nut-and-seed protein bars that Camden was obsessed with. They often sold out of the bars quickly, and Camden got excited when he was able to snag one.

While the barista prepared the drinks Theo had ordered, he started to feel self-conscious. It wasn't unusual for him to buy two drinks. It was especially not unusual for him to buy a drink for himself and a drink for Camden, but never this early in the morning. Would the barista assume he was buying some man a morning-after breakfast? Was it weird for him to do so for Camden?

Surely not. They were friends. And yes, Theo had left Camden in bed, asleep and rumpled from sex. And also, Theo was returning with baked goods because he felt an unexplainable impulse to make Camden happy.

But at face value, that didn't have to mean anything other than that they were friends. Who had had sex. And were now going to have donuts together.

Theo liked face value. He thrived in the face-value realm when it came to his emotions.

Yeah, they were friends, and this was a totally normal way to start the morning.

With that minor freak out behind him, Theo drove back to Camden's apartment. He juggled the box of carbs and the drink carrier as he reached Camden's front door, only to realize he didn't have Camden's spare key on him.

"Shit," he whispered. Maybe he could knock, but that defeated the purpose of surprising Camden with breakfast in bed—a surprise that had appealed to Theo.

The door swung open, and Theo jumped, almost dropping his Bold Brew haul. Breakfast in bed was out, but seeing Camden frazzled and sleepy made Theo smile.

"Hey, thanks." Theo breezed through the door, his hands completely full.

As Theo neared Camden, he leaned to the side, and Camden tipped toward him, and suddenly, their lips pressed together.

A kiss.

A flyby kiss. A hello-good-morning kiss.

They both froze, their mouths a breath apart.

"Oh." Camden jerked back, and his eyes widened.

It was a very different kiss than the ones they'd shared before. Way different than the times their mouths had fused because of desperation and passion. They weren't naked, and there wasn't role play happening or sex or ... fuck. A flood of emotions swamped Theo—confusion, shock, fear ... excitement. He didn't know what to do with any of it.

"Oh," Camden said again. He took a step backwards and collided with a wall. He dropped his phone.

That wasn't good. Camden was smooth. He didn't get

frazzled easily and was always in control, but he didn't seem to be in control now. He seemed horrified.

If Camden wasn't in control, if Camden was *horrified*, then what the hell did that mean for Theo?

"You kiss all your friends," Theo blurted. "I saw you. So it's no big deal. You don't need to make it a big deal."

"What?"

"You kiss your friends when you greet them and when you say goodbye. I've seen you. Stop staring at me like we just committed a felony."

"I do *not* kiss my friends. Not like *that*. I haven't kissed anyone in that way but you in over a year."

Theo didn't want to hear that. He strode by Camden to reach the kitchen. He needed a drink, and a matcha tea would have to do. Though, he'd sell his soul for tequila.

They'd kissed plenty. Theo had no idea why that peck on the mouth had turned him upside down, or why Camden was so dismayed by it.

"When do you work today?" Theo asked. He deposited the box of baked goods and the drink carrier on the counter.

"Soon. What are you doing?" Camden was still standing in the entryway, gaping. His voice was incredulous, and it poked at the insecure parts of Theo. "What is *all this*?"

"I bought us breakfast."

"Why?"

That was a great question. Theo was starting to regret the choice.

He shrugged. "Why not?"

It had felt like a boyfriend kiss. And buying Camden donuts, protein bars, and a sugary drink because he deserved a bit of indulgence every once in a while was also something a boyfriend might do. *That* was why it was freaking Theo out.

And evidently it was also scaring Camden.

Theo didn't know what the hell any of this meant. Yes, he'd been doing sex stuff with Camden, but they'd had an agreement of sorts. The goal had been to help Theo get more comfortable. To help him gain experience so he'd be ready when Camden set him up with Hawke.

It wasn't supposed to feel like this.

Theo found his tea and took a huge gulp.

"We need to talk," Camden said.

Theo turned so they were facing each other, Camden by the door, Theo in the kitchen. Camden's apartment was tiny, but there was a mile-wide gulf separating them.

"About what?"

Camden's face crumpled, and he looked so lost. "About us. Fuck. Isn't it obvious?"

"Isn't *what* obvious?"

Theo could feel himself shutting down. He'd always had that problem during conflict. When his parents had glowered at him from across the kitchen table, barely saying a word but making their disappointment very apparent. When Freddie had presented him with reason after reason for why their relationship had been failing.

Each time, Theo's mind had started to power off, and he hadn't been able to think clearly or articulate his emotions. He hadn't been able to understand his emotions then. He couldn't understand them now.

"We've crossed a line, Theo," Camden said angrily.

"Because we just kissed? That was nothing. It doesn't have to ruin anything."

Camden stalked into the kitchen and flung open the box. Theo saw him hesitate over the protein bars before pulling out a cake donut with chocolate frosting. Theo's favorite.

"I know you're freaking out because I'm upset. But I'm only upset because I'm worried and confused, and we need to talk so badly, but you're blocking me. I *need* you to be able to talk to me. Eat this. You'll feel better." Camden handed the donut over.

Theo hated when people were angry at him, but even worse was how well Camden knew him and the care Camden was showing him despite the anger.

"You want a boyfriend, don't you?" Camden asked.

God, did he? Theo didn't know what he wanted besides to call in sick to work and crawl under the covers for the day.

And to think about that kiss some more, analyze it and understand it better.

"I guess."

"You want to date Hawke Howard. You have a date with him this week."

Theo opened his mouth to reply, but nothing came out.

"Eat, Theo," Camden said gently.

Theo took a small bite, and the lump in his chest loosened slightly. "I have a date. He asked me out."

"And you've had lots of sex-toy practice now. I'd say you're pretty proficient. You've found stuff you enjoy. You can articulate what you want."

Theo had figured out what he enjoyed. He liked the role play and the novelty of the toys. He liked the way Camden could make his mind blank and his insecurities disappear. He'd been more honest with Camden about his desires than anyone in his entire life, even Freddie, but he had no idea if he'd be able to replicate that with someone else. Camden was safe.

What if ... what if Camden was the only person who could make him—

Nope. Not going there. Camden was practically throwing him at Hawke Howard. That was all Theo needed to know.

"Okay."

"And he's a nice guy, isn't he? This was what you wanted."

"I—I ... yeah?"

"What are we doing here, then?" Camden gulped in a ragged breath. "We have to stop doing it if you don't want ... I can't wreck our friendship. It is literally the most important thing to me."

"I don't want to wreck it either."

"Then it's settled."

Theo gingerly placed his donut on the counter. "What's settled?"

His chest felt funny, and his stomach hurt. This was why he sucked at relationships. If he couldn't have a slightly tense conversation with his best friend, a man he'd known since he was in second grade, how was he supposed to handle a boyfriend?

"We can't do this anymore."

"Kiss?"

Camden gripped Theo by the shoulders. Theo knew that the relief of feeling Camden's hands on him again would be short-lived.

"*Anything.* Any of this. No more kissing. No more sex or phone sex or role play. If you need help figuring out a sex toy, you'll have to Google it. There are hundreds of toy-review blogs and sites that will give you the info you need. Hell, there's multiple subreddits too. I should have been pointing you in that direction all along, and I'm so sorry I didn't."

"So, I can't come to you if I need help? I thought—"

The unfairness of what Theo was saying slammed into him. He grabbed Camden's wrists. "No, wait. Ignore that. I'm not being fair. My hang-ups are not your responsibility. I'm sorry if I took advantage of you."

"I already told you—You didn't take advantage of me, Theo. But I don't want to lose you. When you and Freddie broke up, you stopped being friends, and I—"

Theo shook his head, and Camden snapped his mouth shut. "Freddie invited me to his wedding. We're still friends. He likes my pictures on Instagram sometimes."

Also, what the fuck did Freddie have to do with him and Camden and their situation?

"Sex complicates things, Theo. Emotionally." Camden's fingers dug into Theo's shoulders briefly. "For me."

Theo nodded. Sex had usually been complicated for him too, until Camden had made it so easy and fun. "I understand. I don't want either of us to get hurt."

Theo didn't consider himself a very brave person, but he'd sacrifice everything for Camden. Hurting him was unfathomable. Unacceptable.

"You're going to have an awesome time on your date," Camden said, his voice a tad too bright. "I can't wait to hear all about it."

Theo nodded again. He wanted this morning to be behind him. "We should get to work, huh?"

"Yeah." Camden dragged him into a brisk hug, and it almost, *just almost*, felt good.

They stumbled their way through goodbyes. When Theo left, he accidentally forgot his tea on the counter, realizing his mistake in the parking lot, but he couldn't imagine facing Camden again.

A swirl of emotions vied for attention in his brain, but he couldn't process any of them. He pulled blissful numbness over himself like a weighted blanket until he made it back to his apartment, called in to work, and pulled a real blanket over his head instead.

CHAPTER SEVENTEEN

THREE DAYS LATER, Theo's tea was still sitting on Camden's kitchen counter. Camden stared at it every morning but hadn't worked up the resolve to toss it.

Yep, he had an unhealthy attachment to a full, untouched, three-day-old, medium matcha tea. Super mature. He was really killing it in the adulting department that week.

Freddie reached over the table and tapped Camden's forehead. "*Hello?* You alive in there?"

Camden rolled his eyes and smiled. "Yeah. I'm alive."

They were at a trendy wine bar, post tuxedo-fitting. Freddie was making his groomsmen wear bottle-green velvet tuxedo jackets for the wedding. It wouldn't have been Camden's choice, even though Freddie said it brought out the "burnt umber tones" in Camden's irises.

Camden had also discovered that the groomsmen, on

both sides of the matrimonial aisle, were being asked to learn a big, videotapeable dance number as a surprise for Freddie from his husband-to-be. Camden was less than thrilled by the idea of learning choreography, but he didn't have the energy to grumble about it.

All his mental bandwidth was consumed by thoughts of Theo's date with Hawke taking place in Laurelsburg eighty miles away. He'd managed to get the details from Hawke since Theo had been pretty tight-lipped this week. They were going ice skating, which would probably lead to lots of touching because Theo was a wreck on skates and would need help. Then dinner at Olympia Greek Restaurant because that was Theo's favorite, but he only ate there on special occasions. Camden had given Hawke that information, though it had hurt to divulge. After dinner, if all went well, drinks at Bold Brew.

Camden hoped it went well. Truly.

Mostly.

"Okay, Mr. Mopes. What the hell is going on?" Freddie's voice took on an amused, biting edge.

"Nothing."

"You're acting so weird, and if you don't tell me why, I'm going to call Cassie and ask her. Or Theo."

"No!"

Freddie froze with a glass of pinot grigio halfway to his mouth. "Struck a nerve, Camden Ray? Who don't you want me to talk to—your sister or the man you're in love with?"

Camden almost knocked over his own glass. *"What did you say?"*

Freddie smirked. "Ooo, got your attention now, don't I?"

"I don't—I don't know what you're talking about."

"Well, Cassie Ray is your twin sister. She's got gorgeous blonde hair and is whip smart. She's a flight attendant. You've met her, I'm sure."

"Freddie."

"And the man you're in love with ... I'm sorry. I thought you knew. *Ah, well.* Let me educate you. You've known him since we were seven. You've wanted him for ages, but your other best friend, Freddie—that's me—is a big fucking jerk who intervened because he was selfish and not a very nice guy."

Camden closed his eyes and tried to breathe through his shock. He'd had too many intense conversations this week. He didn't think he could handle another.

"You're not a jerk. You loved him."

"I did. But I also knew that I wasn't the only one, and I wasn't the right choice for him."

Camden shook his head. "I don't understand what you're talking about."

"Camden, hey," Freddie said. Camden's eyes flew open. "I was trying to jolt you into paying attention to me.

Not a nice guy, remember? I'm sorry. We don't have to talk about this, but you don't have to keep it a secret from me. I've always known."

Camden was so tired of fighting his feelings, his secrets. "I am so screwed up, Freddie."

"No, you're not. Do you want to talk about this? Because I've been dying to for ages."

"Okay."

"How long have you loved Theo?"

"A long time. It was pretty hypothetical before you guys dated. I liked him, but I wanted to fuck around and party more. We were young. I thought I'd have time later but realized I'd lost my chance after you two got together. I was an arrogant asshole too. At the time, it never occurred to me that he wouldn't want me back."

"And is Theo the reason you're turned upside down now?"

"Yeah."

"What happened? You've been living pretty comfortably in the friend zone for a while."

Camden found himself desperate to share, once and for all, but he couldn't compromise Theo's confidences like that, especially not to Theo's ex-boyfriend.

He scrunched up his nose and sloshed red wine down his throat. He had no idea what kind it was—a wine connoisseur he was not—but it burned and tasted good in equal measure.

Choosing his words very carefully, he said, "Theo has a date tonight, and I'm jealous. Things have been a bit, umm, different between us lately, and it has me confused. We talked about it, though, and we're back to normal. I don't want what happened between you two to happen to us."

Freddie scowled. "That story is so full of plot holes it might as well be swiss cheese, but let me get this straight. You've been *different lately*—whatever that means, but I hope it means something hot—yet, you've decided to stop being *different* together because you've discovered that you're not compatible, and you'll never make each other happy."

"What? No. That's not—"

"That's what happened between Theo and me." Freddie's eyes were far too shrewd, and Camden couldn't help but feel like he'd stepped into a trap.

Camden shook his head. "I meant it isn't worth ruining our friendship."

"I'm friends with Theo. I like his Instagram posts all the time."

A laugh slipped out of Camden, unbidden. "That's exactly what he said. I want us to be more to each other than Instagram followers."

"Yeah, you want to be *soulmates*. Which will be easy, considering the reality."

"I don't know what you mean."

Freddie downed the rest of his drink and grinned at Camden from across the table. Camden loved the guy, but damn, did he want to strangle him for talking in riddles.

"I know you don't. During this period of *different*, did you ever once tell Theo how you feel about him? Because I know from experience that you have to be pretty blunt with him."

Of course Camden hadn't told Theo how he felt. That would involve *telling Theo how he felt*, which was a ridiculous concept. The closest he'd gotten was telling Theo that their sex gave him complicated emotions, an admission that seemed to have caused Theo to shut down and disappear for days. Super great, and exactly what he'd been trying to avoid.

"The guy he's going on a date with tonight is nice. He's successful. He's got a cool house and money and a degree."

"Oh, fuck off, Cam. I really am going to call Cassie to knock some sense into you. You do realize you're hot, don't you? And I'm assuming you're adequate in bed. Also—"

"*Hey*," Camden inserted, but Freddie kept talking.

"You work hard. You smell good. And most importantly, there is not a single person in the entire fucking world who would love Theo as much as you love him. Not a single person who would treat him like you treat him. You have this soft spot for him that is so sweet and inspiring." Freddie peered down into his empty glass. "I wanted that. I wanted someone to look at me the way you look at him. To take care of me, even when I don't need it. To understand me. To help me. You were this shining, scary example of unconditional love, and I was so jealous. So I dumped Theo and went out and found it myself. Because he never looked at me like that, Cam. But he did look at you."

Camden's ears were ringing by the time Freddie finished. His tongue felt too big for his mouth.

He wanted to believe the things Freddie had just said, but it was so hard and scary.

Freddie reached across the table and stole Camden's wine, taking a sip of it. It was so reminiscent of Theo that he laughed.

"You're worried about ruining your friendship," Freddie said. "But being in love with your best friend and experiencing that love in return is the most wonderful thing in the world. Oh my God, why am I not writing this shit down for my vows? You have to help me remember it all. Groomsman duty."

Freddie whipped out his phone and started dictating into it. Camden leaned back in his chair and tried to untangle the hope Freddie had wrapped around him.

CHAPTER EIGHTEEN

THIS DATE WAS GOING GREAT, Theo thought. Or at least, it was going ... fine.

It wasn't as horrible as it could have been.

He hadn't broken anything while ice skating, and Hawke had held his hand to prevent any major tumbles. It was the epitome of romance. He relished the idea of a big, strong man teaching him a thing or two. Obviously. Hence his multiple tumbles with Camden.

Now they were at the romantic-dinner portion of the evening. Theo lifted the last bite of his food to his mouth and tried to savor it. Hawke was watching him like, well, a hawk and seemed to be reading all of the insecurities flitting through Theo's head. Theo knew that was impossible but was also certain it was very, very real. Hawke's eyes felt *too knowing*.

"How was your food?" Hawke asked.

"Oh God, the souzoukakia was divine. Thank you for bringing me here. This is my favorite restaurant."

"Yeah, Camden told me."

"Oh. That was ... nice of him."

"He definitely loves you, that's for sure." Hawke smiled mildly.

Theo blushed as if he'd been blasted with all the heat from the sun. "He's my best friend."

Hawke tapped the table with his fingertip a few times. "It's okay if you love him too. I wouldn't blame you, and it'd be good to know now, before I humiliate myself and fall head over toes for ya." There was a touch of humor in Hawke's voice.

"What are you talking about?" Theo was breathing hard and felt odd. Maybe he was reacting to an ingredient in the melitzanosalata. He'd never eaten it before, and they'd shared it as an appetizer.

Hawke leaned back in his chair and studied Theo. "Just checking."

"Checking what?"

"You guys seem like you'd be perfect together. He talks about you all the time. You couldn't stop looking at him on Monday night. I can't tell if you're friends or if there's the potential for more there. I like you. I want to be your friend, regardless, but I don't want to waste my time on romance if you're emotionally unavailable."

Holy shit, was this how some adults negotiated their

feelings on dates? Because Theo had not been prepared. He'd never been good at verbalizing his thoughts or desires.

"I don't—" Theo shook his head. "I asked him to arrange a date between you and me. I already told you that, I know. But I did it because I'm tired of being alone, and my ex is getting married."

"Go on."

"I was intimidated by you. I, well, you're *you*. And I'd never held a sex toy, and it was a lot to imagine trying to deal with if I ever saw you naked so—"

"God, you're cute. I don't care that you don't have experience with toys. It's not a prerequisite because I own First-Rate Finishes."

"Okay, well ... I do have experience now. Because Camden helped me."

Hawke picked up his water glass and smiled. "*Ah*."

"Why did you say that Camden loves me? How do you mean?"

Theo's chest was unpleasantly tight. All those penetrating stares and long pauses and that kiss at Camden's door with the donuts—they were an equation Theo couldn't quite grasp.

"You've been friends with Camden your whole life," Hawke said. "I think you know he loves you."

"Well, of course he loves me. And I love him. He's my best friend. But I never thought he'd *see* me like—" Theo squeezed his eyes shut. "Shit."

A small sparkle of hope was floating just out of Theo's reach. It was the same feeling he'd had the morning after he and Camden had had sex, when he'd analyzed the curl of Camden's hand and the striations of color in his stubble. It was the feeling that had pushed Theo out of bed and to Bold Brew to get them breakfast.

He'd dismissed that hope as nothing but an inconvenience. He'd shoved it into a box in his brain and tried to forget about it.

Theo had been deliberately compartmentalizing during every episode with Camden because that was what Theo had always done with his emotions. He'd been preventing himself from thinking and feeling, but what if he grabbed onto that hope instead?

Camden *saw* him. How many times had Theo noted that in the last week?

Camden understood him. He cherished him. He welcomed Theo's quirks and eccentricities. He was kind about Theo's insecurities. Camden showed Theo care and love in a million tiny actions.

Camden saw him.

And Theo wanted to see Camden in return.

That was what Theo had been hiding from.

He'd felt like shit after their conversation on Tuesday, had felt rejected and, honestly, a little heartbroken, even if he hadn't been able to admit it at the time. He understood that

Camden was scared of losing Theo's friendship, but Theo had also never articulated, to himself or to Camden, that they could be friends and love each other. The two concepts weren't separate when it came to him and Camden.

"Camden asked me to be his date for the wedding, but I suggested the matchmaking instead." Theo covered his mouth with his hands. "Oh my God. I thought it was a pity suggestion."

"You are many things, Theodore Punch. Pitiable isn't one of them."

"I think—" He glanced around the restaurant. It was intimate and quiet. He enjoyed this place, but it had nothing on eating enchiladas on his couch next to Camden. "I think I've been the worst date tonight, haven't I?"

"Oh, I don't know. Watching your realizations has been pretty fun."

Theo smiled. "I hope we can be friends."

"Me too. Now, as your friend, let's gossip. What are you going to do about Camden?"

Theo took a deep breath, some of the turmoil settling in his chest. Since they'd embarked on this matchmaking scheme, he'd been relying on Camden to step up. On Camden to be in control.

Theo pulled out his phone. It was his turn to take charge. "I've got a plan."

"Good. He deserves to know what's put that hope in your eyes."

——————

THEO WAS able to snag his usual table at Bold Brew after buying himself a tea and Camden a coffee.

He had no idea if Camden would show. He hadn't answered Theo's call, and the text message asking Camden to meet him here had gone unanswered. Theo knew that Camden had gone to a tux-fitting with Freddie and the other groomsmen, so he was probably occupied.

That was okay. If Camden didn't show up today, Theo would try again tomorrow. Or the next day.

The bustle of Bold Brew flowed around him, and he closed his eyes, trying to enjoy it. He liked Bold Brew this late in the evenings. It was full of students studying and hives of social activity. There was a guy with a beard and long hair playing acoustic guitar and collecting tips in the corner of the room. The fireplace made the coffee shop cozy.

If this didn't work, Bold Brew might be ruined for Theo forever.

A few minutes later, a ruffle of fingers in his hair almost startled him but didn't. He knew those fingers. Loved them. Didn't even need to open his eyes to see who they belonged to.

Camden sat down opposite him. "How was your date tonight?"

"Horrible. And wonderful. I got you coffee. Decaf since it's late. I know you like coffee the most, but I buy you oddball things so I can, uh, liberate them from you. I'm sorry about that."

"Don't apologize. I love sharing with you. What's wrong? What was horrible about your date?"

"Hawke's not the guy for me. That was made abundantly clear."

"What did he say to you?" Camden asked through clenched teeth. "Was he rude?"

The reaction surprised and delighted Theo. "He wasn't rude. He asked me if I had feelings for you ... And I do, so that made it awkward." The words were out there now, said in an uncomfortable rush. Theo couldn't pull them back in. There was nothing to do but soldier on. "I do have feelings for you. A lot of them. And they're big and scary and important. I should have recognized what those feelings were before, but I didn't, and I'm sorry. I want to tell you now, though. I love you."

Camden stared, unblinking.

After ages of silence, Theo laughed a little. "Please say something."

Camden's head twitched, side to side, like he was shaking his head *no*, but more involuntary. "I don't know what to say."

"Well ... You don't have to say anything. It's okay that you don't—"

"Wait." Camden grabbed Theo's hands and squeezed. "Hold on. I'm freaking out and don't want to fuck this up."

"You don't need to freak out. It's me and you. Nothing you say is wrong. Nothing you feel is wrong either."

Camden's chin wobbled, and he pulled their entwined hands to his face, using them to hide. "I'm sorry. It's been a weird night."

Alarmed, Theo scooted his chair closer until they were side by side. No one seemed to be paying them any attention, and he hoped their words were drowned out by the plinking of guitar strings and the hushed conversations of other patrons.

"Aren't you scared?" Camden asked.

"Of what?"

"That loving each other will screw everything up. That we'll fracture the Three Mountaineers for good until we're all just single entities, existing without each other, and you'll never talk to me again. I'd be so fucking alone, Theo."

"So you're saying you love me?" Theo asked, a smile playing across his lips. He couldn't help it.

"Of course I love you." Camden released Theo's hands. "Did you not hear anything else I said? What in the world makes you think I wouldn't fuck this up? I've *already* fucked this up. The matchmaking. The sex toys. Hawke. I feel like our friendship is barely hanging on because of what I've been doing, and I cannot lose you."

"*Cam.* Our friendship is not breakable. It's not that fragile. I promise."

"But Freddie—"

"*Isn't you.* Isn't me. Freddie and I broke up because we weren't right for each other. And our friendship fell apart because we were twenty-five, and I was too self-absorbed and preoccupied to fight for it. But I am right for you. *I know I am.* And I will always, always, always fight for you, Cam."

Camden groaned and scrubbed his hands through his hair. "Oh my God, you're going to make me cry in fucking Bold Brew."

"I'm so sorry if I hurt you with the … uh … role play, sex-toy stuff. It meant something to me, in my heart. It was emotionally complicated for me too. But I didn't tell you that. Couldn't even tell myself. I wouldn't have been able to be vulnerable with anyone but you. I don't *want* to be vulnerable with anyone but you."

"I'm sorry too, Theo. I haven't been honest. I've loved you for almost half our lives." Camden laughed, a harsh, tortured noise, and cupped Theo's face between his hands. "Geez, I can't believe I've finally said that out loud. Literally everyone knew but you."

Theo's heart felt too light for his body. He was smiling

so wide his face hurt. "We're going to be okay, Cam. I promise."

"I don't want to be your matchmaker anymore."

"Well, good. I've found me a match."

"I want you to go to the wedding with me." Camden's thumb skimmed Theo's cheekbone.

"I accept. I'll feel like the belle of the ball."

"I want to be able to kiss you over donuts and when we say hello and here at Bold—"

Theo couldn't stand it any longer. He stole the last word from Camden's lips.

He knew the shape of Camden's mouth. Had it memorized. He could picture the way it had changed through the years, his lips filling out, his smile hardening, his stubble growing in. He knew what Camden tasted like during sex, all fire and control and impulsivity.

But Theo wanted to discover him in these sweet moments. The way Camden smiled slightly into the kiss and held Theo's chin tenderly in his hand. The tease and feather-light brush of Camden's tongue. The nudge of his nose against Theo's glasses. The lovely hitch in Camden's breath.

Camden mouthed, "I love you," against Theo's lips, and Theo memorized that too. Unearthed that miracle to keep in his heart forever.

Then he shared it right back, his own heart in his hand. "I love you too."

CAMDEN TRIED to remember the choreography. Freddie's newly vowed husband, Antony, had certainly drilled it into Camden's brain enough in the last two weeks. But as Camden and the other groomsmen circled and stepped and essentially made fools of themselves for *romance*, Camden kept losing his footing.

Freddie was on the threshold of the dancefloor, looking resplendent in a black tux with gold brocade, his eyes full of tears at this incredible gift. That was the only reason Camden had agreed to this groomsmen dance surprise. He'd known Freddie would love it.

"Spin, Cam!" a voice hollered from behind Camden, a most beloved voice. "Get it, baby!"

He peeked over his shoulder and laughed. Theo was making a raise-the-roof gesture, and Camden bumped into

Antony's best man. At least Theo didn't have his phone out recording like everyone else.

"Sorry," he mumbled.

"No worries," the best man said. "This torture is almost over."

The groomsmen ended on their knees in front of Freddie. Antony swept through the middle of them and swept Freddie into his arms for their first dance. So much sweeping.

Camden stood and gratefully hurried off the dancefloor. He was waylaid by Theo, who immediately wrapped his arms around Camden's waist.

It had been six weeks and twenty-two hours since that night at Bold Brew. Camden had been keeping count.

"You have terrible rhythm," Theo whispered, like he was breaking really bad news. He pulled Camden farther off the dancefloor, steering him out of the ballroom altogether. Camden was happy to follow Theo anywhere now that his official duties for the evening were done.

"That's going to end up on YouTube, isn't it?" he said. "The groundskeeping crew is never gonna let me live it down if that goes viral."

"I doubt it'll go viral. That stuff only goes viral if the dancers don't look like a miserable herd of elephants stomping around."

"Charming. Thanks. I worked hard on that. Freddie seemed to love it."

Theo grinned up at him, and Camden dropped a kiss on his lips, catching the brunt of his smile.

Theo pulled them to a stop and wrapped his arms around Camden's neck. "Kiss me again."

Camden would never deny Theo that. He'd spent hours upon hours kissing Theo. Kissing Theo's body—the soft spots that were for Camden's eyes only. The backs of Theo's knees. The ticklish stretch along his ribcage. He'd kissed Theo during the heat of the moment, when both of them were on the edge, when both of them were coming. He'd absolutely ravished Theo's mouth the night before during a bit of repairman/homeowner role play on top of Theo's washing machine.

But kisses like this were Camden's favorite. They were the natural progression of that oopsie-daisy kiss in Camden's entryway six weeks ago. A kiss because they were happy to see each other, to be together. A kiss that meandered with no clear destination in mind.

He nibbled over Theo's bottom lip, taking sips of his mouth. He tasted like champagne and a hint of the tea he'd drunk on the drive to the wedding. Camden cradled Theo's face in his hands and deepened the kiss, chasing Theo's flavor, waiting for his groan, knowing exactly where to touch and press and prod to make Theo melt in his arms.

It happened so fast, Camden barely caught him. Theo shuddered and fell pliant against Camden's chest.

They were in a hallway with patterned red carpet,

elaborate crown molding, and gold-framed paintings. No one was around, so Camden pinned Theo to the wall. At the very least, it helped distribute Theo's weight.

"Hey, boyfriend," Theo said with what Camden now recognized as his horny smile.

"Hi, Theodore."

"Have I told you how sexy you are in that tux? Like a hot blackjack dealer."

Camden pressed his laugh into Theo's throat.

"With me," Theo said, "the house always wins."

"You're a dork."

"Or, oh, I know! I could be a blackjack card counter, and you're the casino muscle who's sent to rough me up via sex and scare me into never cheating again."

That had ... potential. Camden shelved it in the back of his brain for later. It would be better with props.

He pulled back to see Theo's face. He'd been worried Freddie's wedding would be hard for Theo, that it would dredge up memories of hurt or regret, but he'd been nothing but bouncy and jazzed all day.

"You seem happy," Camden said.

Theo blinked. "Of course I'm happy. I'm here with you."

Camden shook his head. He had no idea how he'd gotten so lucky. The last six weeks had been a dream.

They'd had a few hiccups. There were times Theo shut down or got self-conscious about his feelings, and

Camden overreacted in his own head, expecting the guillotine to drop. And there were times Camden was exhausted from his long work hours, coupled with his own insecurities over money and status.

But they also knew each other. Camden knew that if Theo got overwhelmed or felt too vulnerable, then the best thing to do was make him tea and get him some sugar. Theo knew that Camden needed way more assurances about his love and devotion than any person rightly should. They worked. They fought for it every day, and so far, it was working.

"Why did you pull me into this fancy hallway, Theo?" Camden asked, palming Theo's hips. He was wearing a basic gray suit that fit him like a glove.

"Just wanted a few moments alone." Theo caressed Camden's chest, sliding it over the pocket. They both tensed as Theo's palm connected with the small oval inside.

"I bet we could find a location that's a bit more alone than a hallway."

"Yep. I've already scouted, Mr. Blackjack Dealer." Theo twirled out of Camden's hands and disappeared into a room a few steps away. Camden followed him, so incredibly happy he could hardly stand himself. He would forever follow Theo.

The room seemed to be a sitting room. There was a chaise lounge covered in floral upholstery, a closet full of coats and purses, a full-length mirror, and a door with a lock.

Good enough for Camden. He flipped the lock and removed the remote from his pocket. They stared at each other from across the room. Theo smiled.

"How did it feel, Theo? Sitting through the ceremony, the constant fullness?"

"Dirty. Like I was doing something bad."

"You were doing something bad. And now"—Camden pressed a button on the remote—"you've been caught."

The second Camden turned on the Rimmy, Theo's head hitched back like he'd been punched. This was a new form of play for them—the remote control, the wearing-a-toy-in-public. It only worked because Theo trusted Camden so much. It only worked because they could be open with each other.

Camden caught Theo in his arms and kissed the spot under his ear that always made Theo's cock jerk.

"Oh fuck, Cam. What do I have to do to make amends? I'll do anything. I don't want to get in trouble with the big bosses." Theo's voice was strained and breathy.

Camden didn't know exactly what game Theo was attempting here, but he was happy to assist. He had to stifle a giddy laugh first, though. They weren't the best at staying in character, but he'd try. He bit Theo's ear.

"Well, I suppose I could keep it between us. It'd be our little secret. But you have to give me something first."

"Anything."

Camden slipped each of Theo's shirt buttons loose, revealing his torso. Then he unbuttoned Theo's slacks and pulled them down. They pooled around his shoes, which Theo toed off in a hurry.

Camden reached behind Theo and tapped the base of the plug there. "I want you to fuck me with this thing in. But we need to be seriously fast."

Theo's gaze went unfocused and his mouth opened on a soundless moan. Camden could tell Theo was struggling to process the sensations in his body, so Camden decided to help the situation along. He shucked off his own pants and underwear and went to kneel on the chaise lounge.

"Wait," Theo said.

Camden froze and glanced over his shoulder to see Theo pull a handful of stuff out of his suit pocket. Theo rushed over, opened a deck of cards, and scattered them over the cushions of the chaise.

"Oh my God, you planned the blackjack thing." Camden started laughing and couldn't stop. "I thought you were kidding."

Theo shook his head. "I'm not a very jokey person. Too busy counting cards."

A long beat stretched between them before they both fell into a fit of giggles. Theo urged Camden to kneel on top of the crisp, new playing cards and kissed him through the laughter.

Camden's chuckling died when Theo had two fingers and a boatload of lube inside him, opening him as quickly as Camden's body would allow. Which was ... not quickly at all. He should have chosen a different sex act if speed was the goal, but the thought of Theo fucking him while on overload from the Rimmy was too delicious to pass up.

Finally, Camden was ready. He planted his hands on the cards and braced himself as Theo worked himself inside slowly, his cock blunt and powerful. They hadn't done this a lot. Only a few times, and while Camden loved it, it also sent a scary thrill up his spine. He collapsed onto his elbows, crushing and crumpling slick cards with his body weight, and groaned into the cushion.

"Is this good?" Theo asked, holding Camden open and plowing inside. His movements were less cautious than usual, which ratcheted up Camden's own arousal tenfold. "Because this is really good on my end, Cam."

"What's it feel like?"

"Like someone is rimming me while I fuck you. Oh, damn. I'm not going to last long." Theo tripped his hands up Camden's sides, pushing his shirt and tux jacket up his body, and held on roughly.

Heat curled in Camden's stomach, whisps licking over his groin, as Theo tagged his prostate. The cards beneath him began to blur, fuzzy darkness creeping along the edges of his vision. He caught his cock in his hand. It was slick and achy.

"Don't come before me," Camden said. "That was not part of our bargain ... Oh my fucking God ... If you do, I'll have to tell my bosses about how you stole from them. They won't be happy."

Theo huffed a laugh and pulled out. Camden would have been embarrassed about the whimper that escaped him if Theo hadn't turned him onto his back and immediately speared him again.

This was Camden's favorite angle. It was perfect, the curve of Theo's cock hitting all the spots inside him that made him cry out and writhe and lose complete control of himself. Theo knew how to move, knew the right way to press Camden into the chaise and steal his breath with a kiss.

Playing cards flew around them, sailing onto the floor and sticking to their bare skin. Theo's face was flushed, his glasses askew. His hair was a riot around his head. Camden adored Theo's face during sex. The sleepy-eyed, red-mouthed marvel.

"Close, Theo," Camden said against Theo's mouth. "Please, touch me."

Camden had never been one for begging, but he was safe with Theo, safe being wide open and exposed, everything on display.

"I'll take care of you," Theo whispered. He whipped

the cloth pocket square out of his jacket pocket—hooray for half-dressed sex—and pushed it into Camden's fist. "Use this. Don't want to get spunk on your pretty tux."

Camden nodded, unable to speak as Theo fucked him harder. Unable to do anything but gasp as Theo grabbed his cock and stroked it in time to his thrusts.

"*Come on, Cam.* Come on," Theo chanted. "I love you, but ... but this is too good ... And *fuck.*"

Theo smiled when he came, a laugh of joy slipping from his beautiful mouth, and it pushed Camden over too. He managed to catch the spurts of his release with the handkerchief, but he did not manage to stifle his own shout as sensation pulsed through him.

Theo kissed his throat as Camden came down. Once he had his wits about him, Camden threaded his fingers into Theo's curls and lifted his head so they were eye to eye.

"Theo, I better never catch you counting cards in my casino ever again. Because next time, I'll demand a harsher punishment."

Theo's laughter followed them through their rushed cleanup, including a quick trip to his Prius to drop off the pocket square and the sex toy.

When they made it back to the reception, the dancing was in full swing. The lights were low, alcohol was flowing, and the music was loud. No one seemed to notice them as they slipped toward the bar, both in need of some hydration.

Camden had just received his beer from the bartender when Freddie appeared and grabbed their wrists with a claw-like grip. They both jumped and looked at each other guiltily.

"I want a picture of the Three Mountaineers," Freddie said. There was a photographer following him around, and before Camden was ready, Freddie had an arm over each of their shoulders and was cheesing at the camera.

Once the picture was out of the way, Freddie turned to Theo and gave him a huge hug. Theo returned it, a content smile teasing the corners of his mouth.

"I'm glad you're here," Freddie said.

"Wouldn't have missed it. You are going to be so happy," Theo responded.

Then Freddie hugged Camden. He pressed his lips to Camden's ear. "Did you sneak off to screw around with my ex at my wedding reception, Camden?" Camden tensed, and Freddie laughed. "I have never been so proud of you." He smacked a sloppy kiss onto Camden's cheek and waltzed off to the next group of people.

An impossible amount of happiness flooded Camden. He was here with Theo. It wasn't fake. It wasn't an experiment. It was real.

"I love you," he blurted, and Theo grinned. Camden usually blurted it out. The feelings seemed to build in him in such an uncontrollable storm that the only way to get them out was by announcing it too abruptly, randomly, and loudly. Camden was not suave at all when it came to saying those three little words.

But he didn't need to be. Not with Theo.

"I love you too."

He handed his beer over so Theo could take a drink. There was no reason for Theo to get his own. They could share.

"What should we do now?" Camden asked, surveying the room.

"We can dance." Theo fiddled with the cuff of his jacket. "If you want."

Camden leaned back against the wall and pulled Theo in front of him. He wrapped an arm around Theo's waist, and Theo relaxed against him.

"You don't like to dance."

"No. I don't."

Camden kissed Theo's ear. "Then I'm happy standing here. On the outside. With you."

———

If you want a little more Theo and Camden, join my newsletter for a free sexy bonus scene!

AUTHOR'S NOTE

FREE BONUS SCENE!

I hope you enjoyed reading *Perfect Matcha* as much as I enjoyed writing it. There is a free bonus scene about Theo and Camden that is available to my newsletter subscribers.

You can sign up for my newsletter at erinmclellan.com

BOLD BREW SERIES FACEBOOK GROUP

Did you know we have a Facebook Group for the series? Check it out for more information about the upcoming books, teasers, games, giveaways, and more!

You can join the here: https://www.facebook.com/groups/boldbrewcoffeeseries

ERIN MCLELLAN'S MEET-CUTE

I also have a Facebook Group for my readers and fans! Group members often get a first look at cover reveals, excerpts, giveaways, and upcoming release information.

Find the group by searching Erin McLellan's Meet-Cute on Facebook!

WHAT TO READ NEXT

If you enjoyed *Perfect Matcha*, you might also like my kinky So Over the Holidays series. All the books are low-angst, fluffy, sex positive, and full of toys! Start with the queer m/f Christmas story, *Stocking Stuffers*, or the m/m Valentine's Day story, *Candy Hearts*!

THANK YOU, READERS

Thank you so much for reading!

BOOKS IN THE BOLD BREW SERIES

ALSO BY ERIN MCLELLAN

So Over the Holidays Series

Stocking Stuffers (Book 1)

Candy Hearts (Book 2)

Bottle Rocket (Book 3)

Party Favors (Book 4)

Farm College Series

Controlled Burn (Book 1)

Clean Break (Book 2)

Love Life Series

Life on Pause (Book 1)

Life of Bliss (Book 2)

Storm Chasers Series

Natural Disaster (Book 1)

Standalones

Small City Heart

ACKNOWLEDGMENTS

All the cheers and flowers to Edie for her wonderful editing, Susie for her fabulous proofreading, Layla for her genius blurb help, and Cate for the awesome cover art. I'm so thankful to have you all on my team.

A huge thanks to Annabeth for approaching me about this series and Abbie for keeping us all on task. To all the authors involved—it's been a huge pleasure being part of this series with you.

Lastly, hugs and kisses to my family.

ABOUT THE AUTHOR

Erin McLellan is the author of the Farm College, So Over the Holidays, and Storm Chasers series. She enjoys writing happily ever afters that are earthy, emotional, quirky, humorous, and very sexy. Originally from Oklahoma, she currently lives in Alaska and spends her time dreaming up queer contemporary romances. She is a lover of chocolate, college sports, antiquing, Dr Pepper, and binge-worthy TV shows.

www.ingramcontent.com/pod-product-compliance
Lightning Source LLC
Chambersburg PA
CBHW050845180626
46814CB00007B/2634